THE LOVE STORY OF THE PRISONER

Junaid Asif

The Love Story Of The Prisoner

Junaid Asif

The Love Story Of The Prisoner

Junaid Asif

Self Published

Copyright © 2020 Junaid Asif

This is a work of fiction. Names, characters, businesses, places, events, locales, and incidents are either the products of the author's imagination or used in a fictitious manner. Any resemblance to actual persons, living or dead, or actual events is purely coincidental.

Love can happen anywhere

PROLOGUE

Love is like smoking cigarettes.

The one who smokes them knows that they are full of shit and that life was and would be much better without them.

The ones who have left cigarette smoking also feel like shit as they crave for it and battle hard to not give in to their temptation. But once as they give in and again start to smoke, they feel much worse and now along with the deadly poison nicotine, even regret fills up in their bodies.

So both the smokers and ex smokers suffer.

The only ones who don't suffer are the ones who have never touched the deadly weed even once in their lucky lives.

Same thing for love, those who have love in their lives, knows that they were much better without it - Betrayals and Heartbreaks.

Those who don't have love, crave for it - Loneliness and Masturbation.

Both suffer.

The only ones who don't suffer in this love are the ones who don't crave for it and in this world there is no one so lucky until now as each mortal among us is cursed to naturally crave for a different kind of Love. The Creator made us Social beings who long for companionship.

Because the only way the Universe can cease to exist is with Love in the hearts of its people.

But don't you get fooled and carried away by the facts of the heart and its love, as Life is meant to be Suffering, so the same being which has been wired by its Creator to be desperate for love and companionship enters and then even leaves this world totally alone. Such a beautiful tragedy. A tragedy to teach that Life is just a journey, nothing more and less.

But Lucky are the ones who get the Chance and a Suitable Companion to walk through this tragic journey of suffering with Love in their hearts and soul.

At sharp ten o clock in the morning we are all assembled in the make believe drama theatre cum old movie hall of our prison where everyone waits anxiously for the yet unknown to us Movie Star. Five minutes later, an almost intoxicating strong fragrance of a ladies perfume comes first conquering the hearts of us men and then walks in the most beautiful woman in the world. Never have we criminal men felt so weak in our lives. All the prisoners start to clap and hoot on her arrival for the actress Layla Rathod, who comes in with a wide white smile while waving towards us with her long fingers as she comes into the centre of the hall and removes her big brown goggles showing her beauteous dark brown eyes. She looks beautifully tan with just a rose colored lipstick and black lining below her eyes. I always had a crush on her since I saw her in the movies, but seeing her in real life now is just something else. Her dress isn't even well fitted today, still her fuller hips seem to be protruding out as if they can kill us all men lethally with the curve. That's what Love and Lust can do to you. That particular hip bulge on the either side of the women is the most dangerous weapon of hers given to her by nature which she can use to get whatever she ever wants. This is the first time when I see her and fall in love with the brunette woman with a thin pointed nose.

CHARLES

S tanding strong on my feet in the darkness of the shadows and still as a mountain. Below my boots is thin metal floor with tiny circle holes in it. I am looking below on the well lighted ground floor as I on the floor above it in the corner watching through the steel pipe railings. This is a huge canteen of the place. My target sits on a silver table, a chubby big guy wearing a white vest and blue denims with lots of hair on his thick arms, surfing through instagram on his phone and with his greedy eyes checking through a profile of a hot chick who looks like way out of his league. Never ever in his wildest dreams will he get to fuck her, not because he is just too fat and ugly for her, but because a few moments later I will be making sure that he ceases to exist. There is an almost empty plate on the table in front of him from which he just had fried rice. All the silver tables around him in the canteen are empty.

I haven't brought my gun today, just a knife and that too I have kept just in case because I prefer whenever possible to kill with my bare hands. That shit is what I live for. Taking someone's life slowly and painfully with just your hands is where the real fun is. Once you do that, the gruesomeness of it becomes addictive as hell, so yeah I am addicted to granting death to my targets and enemies with just my bare strong hands, enjoying it gradually and as brutally as possible even though I have a great aim and control over any and almost every type of gun in the world.I wait for a while, adjust my black jacket while putting on the hoodie cap over my head and then jump over the railings as I land hard on the table just a little behind him like a superhero. My hard sudden super hero landing from a floor above not only panicked the fat guy shitless as if a ghost just caught his mom, but even hurt my right knee bad. No more jumping from such a long height next time.He almost drops his phone from his hands while turning quickly at my sudden thud groundbreaking sound. He looks at me with wide opened eyes and mouth for a second until the shock goes away and he realizes that maybe I am not a ghost after all, just a human wearing a black hoodie jacket and boots there to murder him.

He gives me a broad smile with his big rabbit like teeth; his smile makes his eyes go smaller. He runs his fingers through the few strands of hair remaining on his almost shiny bald head.

'So you found me huh?' he asks while still stretching his cheeks to smile on which there is stubble beard. Tryig to act with a charm, He has got balls, I can tell you that, to be in a easy jolly mood even when his death is literally standing right in front of him.

I don't answer and just keep looking deep in to his eyes to make him feel the terror of mine.

'So are you going to kill me now?' he questions jokingly as if he is not even a bit scared from my presence.

I jump down from the silver table and start to walk towards him. He looks at my approaching footsteps as he puts his two fat index fingers into his mouth and gives a loud whistle with all the power in his fat lungs. Soon the doors on the either side of the canteen start to quiver as other men way fitter than the one in front of me start to fill the room. Strong gangster men of different sizes and shapes keep on walking in through the doors and soon there are more men then I can count. Pumped muscles and shredded bodies seem like a default feature in majority of them. Maybe they are twenty five I approximate while having a look all around me. Almost all of them have tattoos over their bodies. There are baseball bats in the hands of a few, some have got just a big knife, one even got a basketball and a few more have got some kind of long thin steel rods. But what strikes me is that why the FUCK in the world has that guy brought in a Basketball? Does he really think he would throw it at me to kill? So is that how I the Infamously Feared Serial Killer Charles is going to embrace the unholy death? Due to a fucking Basketball?

Oh there are just three or four men among them that don't have anything in their hands. Good thing that none of them have a gun and bad thing that I didn't bring my gun today. I take a few steps back to adjust my position in the centre of the crowd of twenty five gangsters who for sure would eat me alive if I don't react fast enough. I panic at first but soon realize that this is what I have always wanted and so the universe has served it to me on a silver platter. Careful for what you wish because all your wishes do get fulfilled sooner or later. Twenty six men including the fat guy who is my target and the one who I certainly and eventually would kill. All these twenty six men for me to kill with my bare hands. What a Grand Feast!

LAYLA

There is a stubble beard on his pale face. The tiny green colored dots of hair in the areas on his chiseled jaw where his beard would eventually grow, turn me on always. He is looking at the ceiling with a half cigarette dangling in his mouth with his right muscular arm around me and my head on his waxed well built chest as I rub my hands smoothly on it. He looks at me with his brown ocean eyes then which makes me fall in love with him all over again as usual as we lay naked on the bed under large silk brown sheets. His body is still warm and mine he says is always cold. I guess that's why I always feel a sort of spark whenever we start to touch. But as we go on it feels like my body fully mixes up in his.

A total embrace of the souls it feels to me. He passes me his cigarette which is almost over by now but I still take it as his lips have touched on it and I would love to have it even if the cigarette later burns my lip. We just had great passionate sex, even though he seemed to be distracted the whole time, he kept fucking for at least an hour in all the positions he wanted to. Even though he never openly acknowledges it, more than my lips he loves to suck my fuller breasts and keep his mouth busy with them like a baby for most of the times when we make love. He doesn't kiss me that much, I guess we all got our preferences. He likes to be dominant. Always. What more can you expect from a male movie super star? Or maybe just because he makes me blow him hard in the start, that's why he doesn't like to kiss me and taste my tongue after that, I don't know, everybody got their preferences and dislikes. Men are weird anyway.

I too am a movie star, but not as big as him and am a female. No matter how much feminism there is in the world, here in this movie industry it feels to me that it would still take a while until men and women would be treated and seen equal. A person of my status would easily get any guy do anything for herself. I could be the Boss of anyone, make anyone my servant with that hourglass figure of mine, I too am a popular actress loved and wanted by millions. But here I am, given all my heart to him- Johnny Singh. Johnny has got a big ego and so do I. But I am in mad love with him and he doesn't seem to have the same feelings. He never even told me that he loves me whereas on my lips there is always a song of love for him. Yet he doesn't care, he just likes to have a good intimate time with me once in a while. Atleast he can't resist my body. The most Powerful Weapon in the World is the beautiful women's body is what he says. If used rightly, anyone can be made to to anything. I don't agree with him on this one, but I would be lying if I say that I myself haven't just more than a few occasions used it to get things going my way.

CHARLES

I am nervous, but in a situation like this it is quite normal. Which means you yourself are normal, Alive and not Crazy. The good part is that more than the subtle nervousness I am way more excitedly eager and thrilled to massacre the twenty five men in front of me with passionate love of hateful killing. I am just about to go for my knife hung inside my boots and before I can, a man swings his baseball bat at me. I instantly lift my left hand to defend the bat as the hit hurts deep in the bone of my forearm, then quickly giving him a good hard punch on the face with the seasoned knuckles of my right as he stumbles back. I had already figured out that in this fight where I am heavily outnumbered, I will get only a few chances to hit the guys, so I will have to make the best use of the few chances and maximum damage by hitting as hard and brutally as I can. Making every hit count.

Another one swings an iron rod and I duck down quickly to save my head as the rod passes above me swiftly cutting the air to produce a quick whistle sound. I take the chance and punch him in the groin, he lands on his knees and I quickly pull the iron rod from his hands into mine. Someone hits something wooden on the side of my face and before I can even fall there is someone else grabs me through the torso and keeps pushing through this big room until my back hits a crispy wall hard. He then starts to throw punches on my ribs and another comes to grasp me by the neck. The neck holding guy throws a punch on my pretty face which I dodge like a fly as his fist hit on the hard wall behind my head. I take the iron rod and stab it from above through the guy punching at my ribs below. Stabbing right through the centre of his chest bone, what a satisfying sound the sudden crack of his bone, the passing of the rod through his flesh, the excruciating sound of his groan. The sound would definitely give an orgasm to the Grim Reaper.

I quickly try to remove the rod from his body to use it further as a weapon but someone else kicks me on my abs and another one hits me on the head with a bat. I trip, loose balance and fall on the ground with that hard wooden blow of that bat and soon there are men all over me holding my neck, hands and feet. They start taking chances to hit me. I try to get my hands free but the men keep holding it tight with all their might. I then try to kick, but that too becomes impossible with the wrapped arms of men all around my legs. I still keep trying to kick and fail miserably as for now I can't even move an inch, meanwhile powerful punches, hits and kicks with the purest intention of destroying my body are thrown at me. Things start to get a little bloody and blurry for me with those direct shots to my head, but pretty soon I am able to free one of my legs because of the consistent struggle of mine and then first I kick the men at my feet on their faces, then lift my legs and hit with my knees to the men near my torso and upon my chest. Then I kick the men on my right hand and then go for my knife in my right boot. I take it out quickly before they can again hold me back and I like some ancient Samurai start swinging my sharp metal knife through the flesh of the men holding my left hand. A guy comes again to get hold of my right hand to press it on the ground and I stab the knife right under his jaw opening the fountain of pure blood from it. Another comes for my legs and I while sitting up pierce the sharp knife through the top of his skull.

I quickly get up on my feet and there are still twenty men more around me. That one guy with the basket ball finally now throws it at me which I easily hit it away with the forearm. He must be very disappointed, but he can still go and grab the ball as I am occupied in war with the rest of the men. So a man swings a bat which I catch in my palms as the hard hit of it gives me a strong feeling of burning of the flesh of my palm and while holding it I stab his arm and then quickly cut his throat as someone kicks me behind my knee and someone else kicks me on the face as I fall down again. I lay down as someone kicks my hand with the knife in it which makes me weaponless again. There goes my lovely little knife far away from me. A big guy then sits on my chest while strangling my throat with his one hand and punching my face with his other. I take three punches of large fist and then go ahead to push my thumb fingers in his soft eyes. Blood pops out of his both eyes as soon as I pierce through them, he never ever will be able to see shit after this for sure. My pretty face even though bruised up bad at the moment would be the last thing he would see in his life. He shouts with unimaginable pain and suddenly lets go of my throat allowing me to breathe better as he tries to cover his destroyed eyes with his palms as if they are magical and would heal the destroyed eyes. Of course it wont, falls off from me on his back as I kick him further on the gut to move him away. I don't want anymore of his blood from his sockets falling on me.

A guy tries to hold my right hand and I grasp his long hair and start smashing his face on the hard ground as the tile breaks. Kicks and hits from the bats and rods keep coming on me as I struggle to get back on my feet.

LAYLA

Back when we started, it was just a fling for both of us. We had many flings like that before with many others we wanted, but this time it was different for me. Thats the tragedy right there, different Just for me. I am the fool who has fallen for him and unfortunately he has not. This cold hearted bastard doesn't feel a thing for me. I look at him like the prince of my dreams and he most probably sees me as a prostitute whom he doesn't even have to pay. Here I am pregnant with his child and I haven't even told him yet. I myself found out about it two days back. So the very next thing I did naturally was to call him which he didn't pick up as usual, as he only calls when he is horny and wants to fuck me. Then I texted him that I needed to see him urgently and that I had something important to talk about. So here he is lying next to me after fucking my brains out as usual and he gets up from the bed sitting straight showing his big shredded biceps. I take the last puff of the cigarette and after extinguishing it in the glass ashtray on the lamp table next to me; I too sit up and start to kiss his bare back. He doesn't react, instead he asks coldly

'So what was it you wanted to talk about?'

His tone doesn't seem pleasant, and not even close to a Lover's.

'I...uh...I' I struggle to speak; I still am not sure in my mind whether I should tell him about his child, about our child, how would he react to it? Will it be a good idea? Will he tell me to go for an abortion? Of course I am not going to kill the child in me. Will he then never ever talk to me and never would fuck me? Even though I love him the most in all of the worlds, in the deepest of my heart I do know that marrying him would never be possible, even if he divorces his present wife, then too he wouldn't marry me because he is not the one who is in love, I am the fool who is in love. So for now even if we make love while him being distracted always, its okay for me. At least something is better than nothing. For him it might be just a wild fuck and for me a passionate love.

Not being able to talk to him or see him again would not be possible for me, I cannot endure that and the thought itself gives me chills to the spine. I accept the fact that he will never be mine, but this whatever sexual relation we have presently, I am okay with this. Having to make love with the person you love the most is an unfulfilled dream for many, but here I am at least lucky to get to sleep with him whenever he wants.

'I have to go, come on. Don't waste my time' he almost shouts at me looking with those brown eyes wide open as if trying to show seriousness with subtle anger

'Ummm…nothing.' I answer while shrugging

'What do you mean by nothing? Are you fucking kidding me?' he shouts while getting up from the bed and throwing away the brown silk sheets. He picks up his boxers and while wearing them I unintentionally stare at his biscuit like lower abs as he continues

'So you just lied to me that you have to talk about something important just so that you can get to sleep with me? That's how low you have gotten now, huh?'

He angrily shouts and surpises me as I almost feel like crying. His mean words almost as always tear my soul as if the sex we had was not at all enjoyable for him and it was good just for me.

'You little bitch, do even have an idea how much work I left, to take out time today to come to you here? How much risks I have to take to not arouse my wife's suspicion?' he keeps shouting and I as always breaks into tears and sob with my head buried in my knees. He still keeps on with the shouting

'All the work I left and the risks I take, just to fulfill your lust you horny bitch!?' he says and after wearing his white shirt, blue denims and his heavy silver Rolex he leaves.

I quickly spot at the lamp table to his side of the bed of this hotel room that he has forgotten his cigarette box. I grab it and chain smoke for rest of the day after that trying to somewhat numb my unbearable pain and all the feelings of the galaxies inside of me. Cigarettes do kill, but not just You, but also your feelings, it weakens them momentarily.

CHARLES

As a child I always saw in the movies when the hero gets cornered by so many thugs, never ever they all attack together at once, except each guy one at a time attacks the hero making the fight easier for him. But in reality all coming together too is not possible, twenty five men at once cannot attack and fit together around one guy but only three or four guys at once can. Or maybe five. That's what was happening here, having four men attack at you at once too is a pretty difficult fight and more over there are twenty more men eagerly waiting just after right behind them to fight you more. But here I was enjoying it to the core. Killing is and will always be my first Love. My Passion.

My target, the fat guy keeps sitting on his ass at the table watching and enjoying me getting beaten up and giving a tough fight to the crowd of thugs. He keeps running his palms over his thick hairy arm which would be a bicep for a thinner guy, as I continue to fight.

A thug swings his knife in front of me which I dodge by taking a step back and I collide into a thug behind me who then swings his iron rod for which I duck down causing the swing of his iron rod to hit on the face of the knife guy in front of me. I then hit my head in the abdomen of the knife guy and then hold his arm which has the knife and strike at his forearm causing him to leave and drop the knife as I catch it in my hands, turn around and stab the pointed edge of the knife onto the chest of the guy swinging the iron rod behind me. He falls with the knife stuck to his chest and I grab his iron rod. A thug punches me and I return the hit with a swing of the metal rod to his face and then pass the metal rod through his stomach passing through his juicy intestines. This guy too falls down with the rod stuck in his body.

Another thug taking advantage of the slimness of the time in my hands due to the occupancy with a few other thugs, comes quick and kicks me on the chest with the heel of his shoe pushing me three steps back as he quickly covers my taken steps to then jump and throw punches at me which I block with my elbows. I reflexively go lower to catch his both feet on the ground and lift them with the suddenness of a jerk forcing him to fall over and smash the back of his head hard on the white tile floor. I in return don't give him the thick seconds of time to even fully grasp the pain, injury and the fact that how the hell did his world slid a total upside down in the blink of an eye as I instantly jump and land with my left knee on his mushy face as his skull breaks with the horrendously powerful impact. The sound of his skull breaking is enough to freak the hell out of the remaining gangsters shitless as the tile below his head too gets cracked and slowly red fresh blood starts to spread like a pool of hell below him. I get up and see just seven more men standing in front of me. The rest are all laying on the ground either cold dead or in immense regretful pain.

A thug smaller than me in frame comes with a knife, he is about to swing at me but I am quick enough to grab tight mid air his arm holding the knife and just poke his eyes with my two fingers making him go bloody blind. Then I steal his own knife and stab him five times in the stomach until another one comes ahead with a crowbar. He raises it high in the air while running towards me and before his weapon can reach on my body, I already have my knife pierced on the top of his skull. I try to pull out my knife but it gets stuck in his tough skull as he falls with it.

A guy comes forward and raises his right leg to kick me on the rib. He successfully lands the kick causing me pain, but I don't let his right leg go back on the ground as I catch it tight near my rib with my left arm and then kick his left and the only leg on the ground as he falls cracking and overstretching the joint between his two legs as I have still held his right leg near my rib. Not everyone practises splits I guess. He shouts loudly in overwhelming pain as I let go of his leg then and twist his neck giving him instant and an easy death, ending his suffering.

I then pick up the crow bar near to me and go towards a thug who has his hands already up in a boxing pose to throw at me. Before he can even throw a punch or a jab at me, I have the sharp points of the crowbar in his nostrils as I pull him and run though the room. He cries in agony as I keep running with the crowbar attached in his nose bleeding and tearing it bathing the weapon in his blood. Even the three remaining men start to run behind us in panic over the pile of bodies I have just laid as I finally jump over a table while landing the face of "the crowbar in the nose thug" hard on the shining surface of a silver table. Of course he dies instantly. The smashed up face looks so bad as if it got served to the Zombies for a Candle Light Dinner.

I then stand on the top of the table like somekind of Conqueror and the only three men stand below waiting for their turn. I jump high in the air from the table as the guys get their heads up in awe looking at me with their eyes and mouth wide open, pretty much confused about what to do. I smack a kick while in the air right in the centre of the chest of the guy standing in the middle of the trio and land on my feet as he falls a feet away with force. For sure the impact of my kick from the air was enough to not let him back on his feet at least for a while.

I stand middle with two thugs on my either side, the one on my right punches me almost dislocating my jaw and the one on my left punches me just above my left eye. I soon take back control by first hitting at the left thigh of the guy at the left and with my same hand I hit back my elbow on the mouth of the guy at the right breaking his two front teeth. Then I take the face of the knelt down guy at the left whom I had hit on the thigh into my hands and hit to destroy his ugly face with a hard blow from my knee as he gets knocked out. I then walk towards the guy at the right whose two teeth I just broke and now is profusely bleeding from his mouth and nose. His secone teeth falling is just about to touch the ground as this guy is quite shocked due to the loss of his teeth like his girlfriend wouldn't kiss him anymore and might even break up with him due to his more newly found ugliness. After I reach near this preoccupied with his teeth guy, I first give him a tight slap and then catch him by the collar while dragging him through the canteen. I pull and drag him by the collar of his shirt till my own lovely little knife fallen on the floor which was forcefully seperated from me moments ago, then I pick it up and stab him six times twisting, turning and enjoying cutting his intestines in his abdomen as he drops dead with blood still dripping out from him like a fountain. He shouldn't have been so worried about the loss of his teeth.

LAYLA

I try calling Johnny for the next two days while cursing and blaming myself to not being able to gather enough courage to tell him about the baby. I had my shoots, meetings, interviews and all the work related scheduled stuff cancelled just so that I could sit in my home, chain smoke and drink Wine until I would fall asleep due to the excessive intoxication.

During the time when I would be anxiously awake, I would keep trying to call him and spamming messages upon messages about another meeting. After three days of him not replying to my both calls and messages, I try another foolish idea. I just text him this time

'I AM PREGNANT WITH YOUR CHILD'

What a clown I was to think that after reading this message like the characters of our melodramatic movies, he would just leave his wife and come running to me for his child. He would then respect, love and take care of me I thought. But life doesn't always give you what you wish for. Next thing I know, he has read my message. There is a "seen" below my message but minutes later after that he has blocked my number and all my social accounts. When someone just leaves you on "seen" and doesn't bother to text you further, it hurts. But someone blocking you from all the ways you could possibly contact them even when you have a piece of their property inside your stomach, a whole new life forming, now that's a whole different type of burn.

 Superstar Johnny Singh isn't the good hearted hero he plays in the movies after all. He has destroyed me. He is Super Rich, Famous, Powerful, Dangerously handsome and flirty with almost all the beautiful ladies, would love to fuck every pretty girl he meets. My friends had already warned me about him in the start as everyone in the film business knows about his notoriously infamous affairs. I too was just having fun with him, a good time, just casual sex with a handsome man never hurts, but then if the unexpectedly wicked arrow of love strucks you, you are fucked. If ever I find that Little bastard of a Cupid Angle who struck me with the arrow of love, I would tear him apart and feed his remains to the neighbour's dog.

 For the two whole weeks after he had blocked me totally, I had been more than just a mess. I did not wanted to kill my child, but my continuous excessive drinking and chain smoking after the heartbreak which anyway I was already expecting from a long time had killed my child inside of me. I didn't even need to do an abortion; my ugly habits were enough to murder the baby in my womb. Or maybe it was just and just the mental trauma I was going through due to Johhny's sudden ignorance towards me.

One night I get a terrible ache in my stomach and my assistant Mini directly drives me off to the hospital, the doctor after the checkup gives us the tragic bad news. There is no more life inside of me then. Mentally I am not even in a condition to feel anything more as I am too numb from the pain, sadness and grief in my body up to the brim, there is no more space for anymore sadness.

A week after that when I get back into my senses due to the fact that Mini was making me aware that if I keep on going on like this without any work, then soon I would be bankrupt and totally incapable of affording the luxurious liabilities of my Top Actress lifestyle.

But the bad news was still waiting for me, someway somehow I don't know, but the news of my child being killed inside my stomach due to my drinking and smoking was all over the world. Johnny's name was nowhere in any of the news. I was their only target. They were just particularly pointing out in the headlines that I had an affair with a man unknown to the sources and it was his and my child whom I had killed after that stranger abandoned me. How in the fucking world the news got out, I don't know and I don't even want to know because even then I will most probably not be able to do anything about it in my present condition. The world has been falling apart for me. All the ugly news even though true to the core is still bullshit without the heaviest and juiciest part of the whole story which is that Johnny's name not being in it nowhere. He sure would have a lot of clout in the industry. God how much I wish I could have even given his name to the gossip media, but I couldn't because my PR team has advised me to just call all the news a baseless rumors to restore my image in front of the people. But a rumor or a reality, a news as bad as murdering your own unborn child in your womb can make almost everyone dislike you immediately. Oh and this motherfucking audiences, the common public, so fucking naive. Always so ready to blindly believe anything and just be judgemental about a person even without knowing their side of the story. Bastards love Ugly news about Anyone. Defaming is more satisfying than sex for them.

Even though by now I and my team have cleared my name formally, getting good work like before have now become impossible. All big directors, producers and Actors now don't want to be associated with me worrying about their own image. It's all a fucking business at the end of the day. They say it's not good to judge but everyone is fucking Judgemental. Casting their petty opinions upon someone's character, considering someone to be bad enough and obviously below them even with the knowledge of just the half ass incomplete story. It's just in the movies where the character of the protagonists is as kind as Jesus, but in reality they are just as evil as the Devil himself. In fact they are the actual devils themselves making life hell for everyone here by not even bothering to enlighten themselves with the other half of the facts and stories. Nobody seeks the Truth. Evil Fools.

CHARLES

My target, the fat guy now suddenly gets up from his seat to runs towards me and then bents down. I realize he might hit me at the torso or be going for my legs as I brace myself for the impact, but instead he just falls on my feet, crying and begging for mercy.

'Forgive me! Please Charles, forgive me. Spare my life for god's sake' he sobs violently while holding and kissing my boots. I lift my right leg away from his grasp and keep it on his fat white face. I then even take away my left leg out of his hands and jump. I land with the bottom of my boots' strong heel hard on his face almost squishing it. Three more jumps like that and my target is dead with his skull cracked and face smashed with another pond of fresh blood forming beneath him. Mission Accomplished.

I take out my cigarette packet which seems almost crushed pretty much like the face of my target. Still I manage to take out a less bent cigarette and straighten it by rubbing my finger tips over it before lighting up as I start to walk towards the exit door of the canteen. I am about to walk out the door and in the blink of a second four police officers bust in through the door with their guns pointing at me as one of them shouts

'Get your hands up in the air where I can see them'

Taken totally by surprise, I raise my both hands with my cigarette still clinging to my mouth

'Get down on the ground now. Get down'

I slowly go down and lie on my stomach with my hands back as they handcuff me. I keep smoking my cigarette as one of the officer carefully pulls it out and throws it away. They take me out to their vehicle and before I can realize I am presented to a court of law and a judge gives me a sentence of a Lifetime while taking in consideration all the murders and assassinations I have done as a hit man until now. Public Enemy. Any single digit ahead of it.

The thing was that I already had some what predicted in the back of my head right in the start that if I take more than five minutes in fulfilling the assassination of my target, then if anybody around the canteen hears him scream or sense any kind of trouble, then they would most probably call the cops and then I will have to hurriedly get out before they get here. But the twenty extra men cornering me at once was not at all expected and way far away from the plan in my mind. The fight took long and maybe someone around the canteen might have seen the killings and would have called the cops or anyone in the below floors or in the buildings next to ours or maybe anyone on the streets. When twenty seven men are fighting and are trying to shout and kill, then keeping the noises down is almost an impossible task. My mind even goes with the possibility that maybe the Fat guy sitting on the table watching me beat down all his men would have panicked and called the cops before coming on my feet and begging for his life. Life is unpredictable and full of innumerable possibilities.

Lifetime imprisonment is a Joke. Fuck that judge. I know I will get out pretty soon, not only I want to and I will, but I will have to. Who the fuck would spend his whole life rotting in a prison? I haven't even done any crime, until today I have killed many, but they all were petty to big criminals anyway, I wipe out Evil, so basically I was just cleaning the dirt for the police and the society. Believe it or not, I am a Man sent by God to do his dirty work. Is that what they call Godsman? I do not know, but I was just doing my job of making this world a better place and sending the devils to hell, their home. For that getting a lifetime imprisonment doesn't make sense to me. I will break out for sure.

LAYLA

A month totally unemployed has passed by for me. I had tried hard to give up my drinking and smoking, but at the end not having anything to do at hand has made the task of giving up the deadly stuffs of intoxication a mission impossible. For now the cigarettes and the alcohol are my only friends and salvation as they ease my suffering. Some days out of boredom I just call young model cum male escorts to sleep with. They got good size and are mostly a good fuck. Also since it's me they are getting to sleep with, they become quite passionately dedicated in their love making. But that too has been becoming an unaffordable thing for me. No work has brought me soon to being almost broke. I had to give up all my perks such as the maids and chefs in the house, the PR agency and my drivers. My sweet assistant Mini is the only one stuck around even though she knows that I would not be able to pay her any time sooner The short heighted girl with dark brown hair and olive eyes on her clear complexion is beautiful enough to get a role in any of my movies, but she never got the desire to act. Mini has become like a sister to me by now over the years.

One day after waking up with a dizzy head, cramps in the stomach and feeling like an ashtray, there is Mini standing all dappered in a wonderful grey formal suit right in front of me in the bedroom. My vision takes me a while to focus and recognize her and as soon as it does, I try to give her a broad smile. She at once realizes that it's a fake one. I then instantly throw up on the bed as she stands in front of me watching me in despair as I Keep vomiting. That's what alcohol does to you.

After washing up, she greets me again with a hot cup of black coffee which she has made herself as there are no more maids in my lavish top floor apartment now. At the moment I just want to hold her pretty hands and tell her how much I love her and how grateful I am for her being so good to me even in my this bad time. She's a real friend, she has proved that. But I am just too tired and fatigued to do anything at present. When you are at your Success, the whole world wants to be associated with you, they want you and treat you as if they love you from the bottom of their ugly hearts and would do just anything for you. But when you are struggling or going through your bad phase, that is the time no one wants to be near you, that's when people show their true colors. Mini is the true friend indeed for which I am totally in need.

Sitting on the brown leather sofa of my grand living room and sipping black coffee, I can sense a bit of excitement in her olive eyes as if she has got some good news.

'I wanted to tell you something, umm actually I wanted to ask you something' she says hesitatingly while looking down at my lap which is both in reality and poetically empty. No blessings, no fortune and no more money left in my lap.

'What's it babe?' I question in my low cracked voice

'I have got some work for you' she says just then looking up in my eyes and I sense that there is something more to it

'Wow, that's great. So tell me about it na?'

'Well it's not like the usual ones.' she replies as she again takes a little sip of the coffee like a cute little sparrow drinking water

'It's not for a movie? Is it a TV serial role? That would okay too. That's great babe.' I say with the little excitement which is the maximum I can show at the moment

'It's not even TV' she answers while still holding the mug in her both little palms with pink nail polish. She looks sad, but I know there is no news in the world that could make me any sadder than I am at the moment. From this, anything would just be a step higher because I am at the bottom most. Still I brace myself while asking

'What is it then? A brand photo shoot?'

She again moves her head sideways indicating a no, looking cute like a doll while doing it

'Then what is it honey? Come on tell me, you are making me nervous now' I ask again getting a little restless now

'There is an acting workshop. You will have to go and teach theatre acting and drama stuff' she replies

'Okay, that's not so bad after all. Acting is the only thing I know anyway and teaching that in a workshop, that won't be much of an issue, instead I feel that would be great nah? Giving back to the fucking world! and teaching is a form of worship right?' I say while keeping my empty coffee mug on the glass table in front of the couch

'Yeah, the thing is I tried really hard. I talked to so many guys, that Amit Kumar, Nitin Mishra, I even spoke to Helen. Well no body wants to work with you anymore. All your old contacts, directors, co actors, everyone have raise their hands up on you. Not a single soul in the industry presently would give you work or even work with you' she says the terrible things in her soothing voice and rubs her palm on my arm to comfort me. This is the best part I like about her, she is always direct and doesn't fuck around to make the things sound less harsher than they are. But yeah, she does take her time and slice of drama to reach till that point. Still at the end she would say the harder truths rather than the easy lies. I love her for that.

'We can't blame them; they all got a business to run. Taking me in with the news I have around me would mean losses for their movies if it flops, so there is nothing much we can do about them. Let it be.' I reply with calmness but still thinking about what has been happening with me aches my heart bad, of course I then go for a cigarette and take a nasty long yet liberating puff.

'Exactly, so this workshop thing is what is the only possibility of getting a work until things don't cool down and get back to normal for us. It is like a two month workshop, Twice in a week you will have to teach and then the payment will be not great, but still it would be enough for you to suffice and manage through these hard months at least' she says before I interrupt

'Something is always better than nothing darling right?' I say while pulling out another cigarette from my packet and passing it to Mini and she gets a bit shook for the moment on my this action as I spot her eyes go wide for a second. Not that we haven't ever smoked together before but it has been quite rare and she just certainly wasn't expecting it now, still then she accepts it and I light it up for her as she clinges it to her mouth and she continues

'So I wanted to ask you, your permission, like will you do it?' she says and that's when I feel that there something more to it, something she hasn't yet told me

'What permission, of course I will do it. What's wrong babe, you wanna tell me something?' I ask while taking longer puffs of my cigarette. She too does the same, we both are quite stressed and nervous at the moment. Puffing up the cigarette smoke with such Passion as if there is no Tomorrow.

'Umm, yeah. Actually seeing you like this breaks my heart. I feel so sad for you, I wish I could do more, I am sorry, but this the only job I could find for you presently considering the situation we are going through. The circumstances have got us fucked for real.' she says while almost breaking down as I notice her voice cracking with pain, this time I feel scared for real, because Mini never ever uses the work "Fuck" or any of that sort in her langauge, at least not in front of me as far as I know, so she saying fuck means we are actually quite fucked this time.

'It's okay darling, don't be sorry for me. I love you so much for even finding this job for me at least. We will get through this as we always do' I answer trying to encourage her and myself knowing fully that in times like these we would ourselves have to be strong to pick our fallen selves up.

'Okay, so I really want you to do this job, the thing is that you will have to teach the prisoners at....umm..at the.. Byculla jail." she says and then takes a pause looking up at me checking for my reaction. I almost curse in frustration, but then I choose not to show my aggression. Going through an unsuccessful bad phase in your career often makes you humbler than ever.

She notices my long deeper breaths I take to keep my calmness as she continues

'Please Layla, this will be good for you I promise'

I have become so much used to making my eyes go wide again and again on hearing about totally unexpected surprises, I do that again while taking another deep breathe and then stop with it because then a thought strikes my mind that I have been going through such an unlucky dark phase, that right now there is a very high probability of some rare deadly particle in the air getting in my wide opened eye or sucked deep in my nostrils and pass into my airways to kill me. Mini talking again pulls me back into my zone of concentration as she asks again

'You will do it na? please?' she sweetly asks like a school girl

I look at my thin hands which are shaking a bit and then at the cigarette in my hand. The smoke of it looks so artistic and as pretty as death and as the paper of the cigarette keeps burning, there are black thin lines of it first on the paper which looks like veins and for sure my veins in the body at the moment would be like the burning thin lines of the cigarette paper. She asks the same question again and I don't reply, instead I just nod my head which gives her a sigh of relief. I still have my gaze fixed at those black deadly veins of poison as tears start to drop from my tired eyes and slowly slide through my cheeks till my neck as I puff my cigarette just thinking

"How did I get so low?"

STORY OF JOHNNY SINGH

Johnny obviously wasn't always Johnny, he was named Janaardhan by his parents when born in their village back in Punjab. It was only at the age of 24 when he officially and legally changed his name to Johnny on the goodwill insistence of his agent thinking it would help in getting movie parts, make a better impression on the casting people in the auditions, be easier to pronounce, remember and sound way cooler than Janaardhan. The agent moreover to convince him, pushing off the edge said that this name would even be better suitable for a Youth Centric Worldwide Brand name in the future. Even though the last part about Worldwide brand sparked the glitter in Johnny's eyes that day while sitting at his agents small shabby office at Andheri East, he still felt offended and an insult to his real name "Janaardhan" about which he was always proud of until then. But he chose to not show his ugly offended mood as by now he was actually tired and desperate searching for a good break in the Film Industry or even just a "b" of a break would do. Anything at the moment that would row his boat was okay with him.

And months later the name change did start to

show its magic somewhat, but it was Johnny's relentless dedication and out of the box unortho- dox choice for scripts that made him the estab- lished star he became later. All the time his only demand would be the GREATEST SCRIPT, even if the director is a newbie first timer or someone with not much experience or some fading dir- ector whose recent movies were a failure at the box office and a total bomb or the production budget and the studio is a small one, if they got the right script to start with, they start with. Even after becoming an A-Lister movie star, Johnny still prefers working with petty budget nobody Independent filmmakers only and if Johnny thinks he has the Greatest Script in the world. Both the audience and the insiders of the industry under- stand his this approach and sincerely appreci- ate and respect it. So even though always trying something New and Unconventional in his films is a very risky affair, the tide mostly turns out to be in his favour.

He is one of the highest earning moviestar in the world, yet he says he charges not a penny for work- ing in the films. He is actually and truly dedicated towards his art. He is the most ambitious and pas- sionate film person anyone would come across. But he produces the film on the back end plus gets to keep all of the hefty amount from the Televi- sion and Satellite rights and obviously the greater percentage from the amount the movie makes at the Box Office.

As a child he would assist his father in farming some days in their long beautiful heavenly fields when not busy with his school work. They would every night after dinner watch Bollywood films on their Grey Heavy Box Television before going to sleep. At that impressionable age, Janaardhan Aka Johnny would feel the world of movies from inside that Old Television pulling him magically into them. He instantly knew he wanted to become like those Heroes in the Movies who would romance the Milk skinned, Long Hair, Beautiful curvy bodied angelic looking Heroines. Even though the actresses with their provocative dresses and bodies of a Goddess in the films would make him go crazy, he would still always be careful enough to not show in front of his whole family of six as they watched the films together.

After his schooling he insisted and made his desire clear to his parents that he would want to go to the City Of Bombay to pursue higher education and a degree in Engineering. Even though the real reason he wanted to come to Bombay was to become an Actor, but he was clever enough to understand beforehand that his orthodox parents with their narrow minds won't be able to comprehend his larger than life dreams and would not allow him to leave Punjab to go and Struggle to find film work in Bombay. So stating that Engineering colleges in Bombay would qualify him enough to get him a high paying white collar job later was strong enough to convince his father to sell one of his three tractors to provide the money for the education and stay in the Country's most expensive city.

Engineering and Engineers had a good reputation in his village as the Old uncles and Gossip aunties chatting to pass their times would often speak about the Son's of the people of their village who had went to other cities to get a engineering degree and then a job, would years later come back and buy more two or maybe three houses and more acres of land property here in their village with the wealth they had acquired from their profession in the city. They would even be married to the prettiest availabe girl of their village and the colourful marriage ceremony and festivities of three days would be the grandest of all. The parents of that Engineer guy would be the proudest on those days with tears of immense happiness in their eyes. "Kinni Soni Kudi Mili mere munde nu"

Money does Talk.

But that's nowhere about the infamous reputation of working in the movies and becoming an actor.

Every single person in the country or atleast in Johnny's village knew the destination of the World of Films, Bombay. Anyone you could ask, a guy repairing the tyre of a cycle, an old sick man on his cheap bed made of rope and wood having a hookah outside his house, a lady covering half her face with her dupatta cloth and going to the river with her mud matka pot to fill water in it, a useless teenager guy squatting on the floor aside the street and smoking his beedi while staring lustfully at the seductive beautiful women at the market, anyone and all of them would know the answer to the question that to get work in films a person would and should go to the City of dreams - Bombay.

But the thing was that everybody had a story where a friend of theirs or a friend of friend had gone to Bombay all motivated and ready to conquer the film world thinking himself as the Next Big thing in the industry, the next Superstar whom every director would want to sign on for their film, whom every actor would like to work with, whom every actress would like to go to bed with, every pretty girl would like to go down for and whom everyone would want to watch on the large silver screens of the cinema halls by spending their hard earned money, but then in actuality nobody in the film world would give a flying fuck about them as there were anyway millions of nobodies like them coming to the city everyday in hopes of making it big in the films. Then these nobodies with their broken heart and dreams would soon come back to their village as a loser after they had exhausted all their savings which they had taken with them while coming from the village initially

Every one thinks of themselves as much better and superior to others, that's a natural thing to feel, so these innocent people go to Bombay with their innocent dreams of making it big in this cruel industry thinking that at their first audition itself the casting people and the director would be astonished by their good looks and superb natural talent of acting. But all the things above are at the end of the day just some pure innocent childish thoughts. So unfortunately and logically all these things Never happen. But yeah, dreams here and all the things do get fulfilled, but that's just once in a bluest moon. Only one guy gets a good part and in comparison thousands of guys never bag a role in their lives. Only one guy would become a leading man in the movies and later maybe an established Superstar and in comparison Millions of guys would fail and go for infinite struggle to make ends meet. All the ones who would fail would either return back to their hometowns dissapointed and embarrased to show their losing faces to their families with whom they had fought to convince them of their decision initially to leave home for Bombay to pursue their movie dreams. Often it would happen that some of them wouldn't even gather the courage to return home and face their families with their failures, so they would choose to not say anything to their families and instead just find some other job or work in the

Bombay city itself and start living their lives here, yet at home they would always say till years that they are still working in the smaller movies and Tv serials or ads.

So when Johnny arrived in Bombay and started to give auditions at Andheri Versova for all the movies, ads, tv serials, he was astonished at the fact that the casting directors and everyone didn't just fall at his feet awed by his over the top cliche acting. He had expected that a person as good looking and talented as him would pretty easily and quickly get great movie roles lined up for him just after a few auditions. The casting guys and the directors at the auditions had been seeing millions of people like him every year who were ambitious enough but looked average or ugly and didn't knew shit about the divine art of Acting. In fact in those long tiring lines of Audition outside the studios, there were far better looking, Insanely talented and deserving guys than Johnny. But Johnny was self obsessedly naive and foolish enough at the time to notice the obvious that the other guys were better built, had a great physique, a better technique, were trained in acting professionally, and so obviously had better chance and deserved greater opportunities. But even they were finding it hard to get consistent quality work and knew that soon they too would start struggling to make ends meet if they don't get that Big Break in the industry. So unsurprisingly to Johnny's surprise he found himself running for innumerable auditions for endless months and didn't even score a part or got any call back.

It was only after 2 years and 4 months since his arrival in Bombay and giving auditions relentlessly without any results meanwhile taking a part time job as a Salesman at a Local Sweet Shop and moving in a small room apartment with nine other strugglers like him living together, that he finally got a call from a studio to come and give another round of audition for a role. Luckily this time Johnny did bag the role as he had by now been working on and developed a good acting technique thanks to the lessons of his roommates who too were struggling actors. The only reason Johnny got the part was that luckily his appearance matched in everyway the physical look demand of the character the show makers were searching for. The role though was just a small two days character part in a Tv serial and Johnny did do it with all his heart. He did get a payment of Rs. 4000 for that 2 days work but then again he didn't see any Acting job for a while. The main actress of that Tv serial - Nikita was a very attractive broad who though didn't have a big bust or something, did have a great looking ass and hips fuller enough to get any man drooling over her along with a thin waist and a very pretty innocent looking face to compliment with. She didn't knew shit about acting and didn't have no desire to even ever learn it.

Everyone on the set would once in a while hit on her and she would handle it with a childlike innocence and so casually yet smartly since it was all a usual thing for her. Even though she was a new comer in the industry and had just done a few acting roles, she still had a reputation of getting too friendly with her male co-actors and directors. But only with the ones who were way ahead of her in the career ladder and status, the ones below her, even if they would promise to bring her the moon, she wouldn't give the slightest fuck. So her open mindness and easy to get laid approach with the biggies of the industry was one of the main reasons that she had so quickly bagged the lead role in this Tv serial while not having enough acting skills. She was screwing both the lead actor Rakesh Mihir and the director of the show, plus she even had one of the producers of the show on her lease. She was friendly enough with the producer but not friendly enough that he would easily take her to bed now. She would only use him when in need, he was her "just in case" things began to get out of hand for her. A clever little woman she was.

So Johnny not knowing any of the inside gossip about her and the industry, obviously got hit by a thunder just by looking at her enter the sound stage that first day where she wore a tight pink indian traditional kurti as the costume for the shoot, her body looked as if exploding from her dress and there was always, unknown to her, so much a sexual energy being radiated out of her. Johnny instantly fell for her and the way she moved through the studio, the movement of her hips made him go mad. After the shoot that day Johnny confident as he always was, tried to approach her as she was reading and going through her next day script seated on a plastic chair at the corner of the set while sipping her Cold Coffee. He first complimented her for the way she acted the scenes that day and she looked up to say a polite Thank You, he took a pause and she got back looking at her script, then he even complimented her about her appealing looks and she again politely thanked him, but even then foolish Johnny kept on speaking and didn't knew when to stop, love and lust makes us stupid. So finally the Actress got up, ignored him and went inside her Vanity van. Johnny felt a bit offended and heartbroken at her this behaviour although she wasn't wrong to do this as everyone always wanted her, she couldn't possibly be available to everyone.

 The Next day too Johnny even though angry at her for ignoring his advances the previous day, still fell more deeply in love with the appearance of that actress Nikita. In his mind he almost forgave her. Then after the two days of that shoot, he went back to his job at the sweet shop. It was again another long gap without any acting job and this time Johnny started to get nervously desperate. But his roommates who too had been going through the same phase for longer time now, motivated him and each other with the moral support that they would eventually succeed and get through. Most of the nights after that Johnny would still think about the beautiful Nikita both before sleeping and even in his dreams. He wasn't the only man having wet dreams about her Angelic Body. He was so crazy for her, somedays he would jerk off just thinking about her.

Seven months after that, Johnny's friend got him a very small character role which wouldn't even have a dialogue. They would mostly probably be a part of the crowd in a scene. Extras. That was their last and only option since that way they would still be close to the sets of Film City, people of cinema and would also get a meagre earning of Rs. 500 for the day. But luck had something else in the box for Johnny that day.

There was also a shoot going on at another Sound stage of FilmCity for a T.V series whose main lead actor even though a Young man in his late 20's just had a heart attack and passed away the following morning. Now the makers of the show were desperately looking for someone to accomodate the occupancy of the main lead. The Producers were putting pressure on the Directors as the T.V serial episodes are always produced in a huge quantity as they have to be telecasted every single day. They are always on a tightest schedule. There is a commitment given by the producers to the owners of the Channel on which the shows are telecasted. Lots of money would be on the line if the shooting of the show doesn't happen.

As fate had it, one of the Assistants of that show came across the sets on which Johnny was working as a background extra, dressed as a part of a village crowd. Johnny caught the eyes of that assistant and then the assistant called there one of his Superior Directors and Johnny finally got a good role. Turns out that the lead actor who died in the morning due to heart attack was pretty much similar looking to Johnny in appearance and facial features. A little bit of clever makeup and touch-ups along with a bit of CGI would be enough to make Johnny look exactly like him in front of the camera. The sound engineer would try his best to edit and match his vocals like that previous actor as much as he can. It was as if some kind of miracle for both them and Johnny.

Soon the makers of the show made Johnny sign a quarterly contract and the best part about all of it was that the main lead opposite Johnny in this show was Nikita. Ofcourse she didn't recognize him from the last time he had approached her, but Johnny even though he was still attracted like a baby to every inch of her body, immaturely still remembered the way she had ignored and insulted him as a nobody. So he did take her to bed, but it was only after two weeks of shooting at work on the sets everyday that until then they kept talking, getting to know each other and then when they got close, he fucked her brains out. Johnny was so passionate and intense as if there was some kind of a war going on between their sexual organs. Nikhita moaned and did enjoy it, but moreover she was surprised at his aggressiveness. Johnny loved making love to her, it was the Finest and the most overwhelming feeling to get to fuck someone you have been so badly attracted to for so long, but back of his head he was trying to fuck her with all his might to punish her for that one time she had insulted him which she didn't even remember now. He never told her about that and soon he did forget and forgive her for that as they through out the time the show ran on Tv they got more closer and went to bed more often. More passionate fucking.

After that show there was no turning back for Johnny both women and career wise. Soon months later he got a good supporting actor part in a big budget movie for which he even got a nomination in the awards for the fresh face new comers. He didn't win it though, that award is particularly reserved and just meant for the new Star Kids who enter the industry through Nepotism. He got appreciation from a few critics though. He bagged a few more side role character parts in other movies and successfull ventures. Soon enough he was casted as the main lead of a low budget feature film which had very less facilities, equipments, production value and was a small crew affair. The thing that made Johnny sign the film wasn't his desperation to become a lead man but because the Script offered to him before hand was something totally unique and never tried before concept. It was about a person who doesn't have one leg which he looses years ago in war in his service to the army and then even after such a magestic sacrifice again when his country is at war, he tries his best unofficially to help the team of soldiers of his country to win. He struggles and passes through all the mountains of obstacles selflessly even with his disability just for the sake of his motherland. Yet he fails in his mission and his country loses the war. Later he is framed and wrongly accused mistakenly as a traitor by his own country and executed. He dies with a content smile on his face though in the climax of the movie thinking he would be more than happy to give even his next and every life he gets for the sake of his loving motherland. The whole movie was a melodramatic affair, but the climax was so perfectly executed by the realistic performance of Johhny, the top grade work of the technicians, the magical vision and direction of the director, the extra sad pitch composition of music by the music composer and the "heart touching and breaking at the same time" dialogues of the script writer that it made even the hardest of men who hadn't cried ever and even through this whole movie drop a few tears over their hardened cheeks. Who ever saw the movie was magically touched by it and loved it. But alas, those "who ever" were only a very few people.

The film was shot on both a tight budget and schedule. The makers didn't even have enough to promote it extensively. Because the film was related to Army and the war, the shooting of principal photgraphy was a tough affair. But Johnny's character in the movie had a wife and another beautiful co-actress in another role helping him in few of the scenes. By now Johnny had become smartly charming enough in this industry and he did make sure to fuck both of them many a few times after packups of the day.

The film finally just released in very limited theaters and the critics praised it to the core. It was an artsy film with lots of heartfelt emotions. Still the film tanked at the box office, didn't do any great business and the makers of it suffered a loss. But Johnny's career after that took a big jump, he got offered more out of the box unique scripts which were this time even big budget productions.

Five years down the line, Johnny was among the top stars of the film industry with two hits, three superhits and one blockbuster movie to his credit. The audiences were loving every bit of him and his choice of work like never before. Till now he had had many a both short and long affairs with many of the beauties of the industry and none from the longer ones lasted more than an year.

He had made a reputation until now of fucking anything that looked pretty. He was one horny bastard of a Superstar who wouldn't mind screwing even a low paid background dancer from the last of the lines if she was beautiful enough for his eyes to get attracted to her body.

It was then that he signed a film with Layla Rathod and lustily fucked her brains out enough that she fell in love with him religiously.

Johnny always had a weakness for pretty women, back in his village too he would just get crazy and smile contentedly with all his heart on the sight of a good looking girl. He would always get horny a bit too quick. But as fate had it, he never had a woman until he was a full grown 24 year old man. And that first time too was upon the insistence of his friend and the uncontrollable sexual urges that he got a very cheap Rs. 300 side of the street hooker who was a middle aged lower than average looking fat woman in a saree. There were several of those type of poor prostitutes all around the streets of Bombay. Fucked way too many times, not that young or good looking and very cheap price they would charge as majority of people living there anyway wanted to get things as cheaper as possible, there were very few who cared enough to give a damn about Quality. It was their job, their institution, their temple, their business -

their body. After all Everyone's got to eat.

Johnny obviously didn't find them attractive at first, but the wild urges of the man turns him crazy into an animal. So he was losing it gradually and decided to give in. It was not that Johnny had never tried with other beautiful women, he always had been trying to date, to get close to them since he was 13 years old, but there was something about him which even he couldn't figure out that made him replusive to women. None ever liked him back. Ever.

None of the ladies found him pretty enough. His school was a complete boy's wing. So never there was a friend or a woman in his life until he was 24 that he then started to get famous with the gorgeous ladies of the Entertainment industry and that also only after he started to get lead roles. No one in the industry fucks people below the line. An actress won't fuck a junior artist or an assistant director, but will certainly spread her legs for the Director and Main Lead if she finds them attractive or worth fucking.

Soon Johnny just within a few years was being ranked by the audiences as the most handsome and goodlooking actors of the lot. He even was being considered for the award of the sexiest man alive, though he didn't win it, it still got him more female attention within the industry. Like the guy who hadn't had a woman to fuck till he was 24 was now having the Power to fuck any top heroine and model he wished. None of them would refuse him, moreover they would be delighted to be screwed by such a big star and also one of the most handsome man in the world. That way these actresses could start and keep a good casual relation with him and then maybe later someday ask him for a favor when needed. Having rich and powerful friends never hurt anybody.

Money does talk and in a quite stylish accent. Johnny used to spent a godly amount of his massively accumulated wealth on his looks, dressing and grooming. It was only now after all this years that he became so rich and successful in such a short span of few years within the film industry thanks to the consistent success of his movies, that everyone loved him, wanted to be associated with him and thought highly of him as a very talented and a charming personality. The same people just five years back would have spitted their Tobacco leaves on his face if they would have seen poor struggler him walking on the side of the street looking for a job. So this people and the World was just now starting to believe in Johnny, but he himself had been always believing in himself religiously. He always since a very small age knew that he was way smarter, more talented and better looking than any average child. Even if he would fail in the tests or any exam, he would still believe that he was the Best. Even if he wouldn't get any girl in the village to accept his proposals or dates, he would still believe he looked the best and the most handsome man in the world. Even his father used to say to him that he looked no hero and just kinda funny, that too wouldn't deter his belief in himself.

So Johnny gave this speech about himself believing in himself since the start, on the stage of the Filmfare Award show after he won the Best Actor award the second time in a row that year. He proudly that day on the stage taught everyone the lesson that the whole world would eventually believe in You, but only if You yourself believe in you for long enough.

Though lots of the famous stars and industry people while sitting in the audience felt not only jealousy but also a lot of anger and contempt at this, after his speech everyone clapped and gave him a big round of applause as if they would always support him till the end of the line. They were all Actors and Film people after all. And Johnny did understand all that. He knew that these people weren't the one who would give a hand to pull him up from the edge of a cliff if he ever falls, but instead they would be the ones kicking him off further to his destruction if they got the chance. But even that they would do with that particular practised fake smile of an actor on their faces. Still, Johnny never felt sad thinking about the fakeness and the double or triple faced people of his industry, instead that day he was too happy when some other thought crossed his mind.

It was the analysis he quickly made looking frkm the stage that atleast more than half of the gorgeously famous divas dressed in their magnificent red carpet designer costumes sitting in the audiences looking all dolled up, have had a taste of his weapon. Johnny almost felt a tear of satisfaction in his eye by thinking about it.

The 24 year old virgin boy Johnny would be so haply knowing about this Playboy Stud Superstar Johnny.

CHARLES

I have to get out, no matter what. It's been two weeks at this Byculla prison and I have hated every second of it. I have got no friends in here; the thing is that to make a friendship in here you got to make an effort at least and I have not done even a bit because I don't care honestly. They hate me most probably I guess and I am okay with that because for the two weeks until now I have been busy in just observing every immaculate detail of the infrastructure of this prison facility. The food here is bad, the other criminals look at me with fear and disgust as if I have killed their loved ones which obviously I have not or maybe I might have since I have killed a total of 489 men including that recent canteen streak of mine.

But more than that everyone here fears an inmate named "Raaga". He is like the unofficial boss in here, of course huge and have got that cliche dangerous looks which the villains have in the movies. But there is a certain Coldness in his "dark as hedgehog brown eyes" that could give any person chills, but not to me. I ain't afraid of nobody, I have personally faced the death herself too many a times. A part of me feels that death herself by now might have atleast a little fear of me.

Here the majority of the stupid prisoners sort of worship Raaga out of fear, thinking that licking his feet might help them in not getting crushed at the hands of fate and misery in this prison hell if incase the circumstances change for them. He has got big heavy arms, dark thick curly hair and a stubble beard always groomed as a impeccably perfect line at his jaw and cheeks.

During the walking time of us all prisoners during the late noons in the huge prison courtyard, we all would merrily keep walking and take a break once in a while, many of them would walk in a group of 2-3 and chit chat like buddies, but Raaga would just often sit there after his intense workout and then his men both puppets and puppies would give him a good oily massage. He would be sitting on a khatiya bench shirtless and all pumped up due to the workout with the minimal equipments and weights specially brought for him by the prison guards. This facility of working out is solely available only for Raaga. A guy at his either hand and feet and one behind him to take care of the massaging of his back and head.

Not too directly, but even the guards here respect him and I can sense a certain fear and agitation even in them. They always are lenient with him and make it easier for his sidekicks to smuggle contraband items just and only for himself. They know about it, yet they never bat an eye. But if even by chance ever they catch any other person trying to smuggle something inside, they not only destroy that particular item or keep it for themselves but also beat him to pulp.

The prison guard's behavior with me is more strict and rude as compared to other inmates. As the tragedy has it, my Boss Karim Laala also cannot help me in here. I have been working for him for over eight years now, killed each target he told me to without ever questioning, and now he can't even get me out from this place. Well he always did pay me well upon fulfilling the killings successfully and I don't blame him for my imprisonment. I totally deserve this punishment of mine because I hadn't taken my gun that day and instead of just shooting my fat target from the distance and running away fast, I just jumped there barehanded like a movie hero to kill him face to face which was a pretty foolish decision. In our hit men business, If a guy gets caught by the cops then he is just considered gone. No help for that guy from that point and I unfortunately got caught. Rules are rules. All us killers know the rules of the game that if caught then you are on your own and there will never ever be no help after that, no relations shall be seen with the gang and the bosses and we are not supposed to rat on anyone. Just shut our mouths about anything, that's the golden oath.

The cops unofficially some days at night after the other prisoners are asleep, do try to chain me up and painfully torture me to ask about my Bosses and the other hit men, which obviously I never answer to, no matter how hard they go on me. They too don't try a lot as they already know that we hit men would never rat on others. We would actually rather prefer going to our graves.

So then since my arrival in this shithole prison, I have done enough speculations on my part and now I have made an escape plan.

One afternoon, the lunchtime where we all would get into long queues with thin steel plates to get the "thinner than water" type of dal, some over cooked roti breads and "tasting like shit" white rice every fucking single day, so the hour before that which is the walking time where we all prisoners in the big open courtyard of the facility take a walk, that is when I go and ask a hawaldaar standing at a corner

'I need to pee'

'No! Take a walk bhosdike' he orders

'Please its urgent' I try again

'Just do walking you maadarchod, go' he replies more strictly while raising his baton stick to scare me off

'Yaar please, understand. I have got kidney problems, I really need to pee now' I say while making sad pitiful faces pretty much like a kindergarten student asking his lovely teacher to to use the washroom. Quite sure, on this particular expression even the cruelest man would feel sorry.

The guard seems a little confused and just looks at his side for a while, thinking

I wait patiently in front of him while keeping on my pitiful expression, my palms over my dick to show urgency as I keep jumping a little bit and making new noises now and then. I should have tried for acting in the movies.

'Oh oh please' I cry gaining confidence in my act

'Okay wait' he says and then goes to speak to another guard a little away on our right who looks up at me from his place after listening

The hawaldaar guard then comes and takes me with him to the pee booth of our prison which is at the inner backside of the building. He waits outside as I go in to take a leak. So until now everything seems to be going according to my plan. There are twelve peeing booths which is six on either side in our toilet where we have to stand and just pee on the walls in front of us. No water after that to wash the penis. There are thin cement dividers between each of the twelve booths to separate them; at least there is some privacy there.

So at the top, high above a wall of this empty toilet there is a window like space for ventilation in which there are vertical metal rods fixed to avoid anyone from going through it. But at the right corner side of this window space there is a gap a little bigger than the gap space between the other rods.

 So first thing, I manage to climb carefully on the second last corner most thin cement divider and then luckily I get hold of the bottom end of the window space. I cling on to it for a while and then pull myself up with my arms. I try to fit and adjust myself through the right most corner gap of the window space between the rod and the wall as I first put my hands out, then my head, followed by my chest and torso I hold the metal rods of the window space from outside to keep my balance and to not fall. Then I carefully take out my right leg and then finally my left leg. The ground now below me looks much deeper from up here as I had expected it to be when I earlier saw it from inside the window space of the toilet. The height could break my bones, any bone if I don't land properly. This is at least the triple of what I had jumped at the canteen for that fat fuck bastard. But now is not the time to think and not at all the time to give up. Never let the fears of the mind overcome. So I close my eyes, take a deep breath and leave my grip on the rods. The sudden pull of the earth's gravity is way more brutal and strong than anyone can imagine and can only be realized when you actually give yourself totally to the air, in that moment you lose total control over yourself and the air speaks to you in its most deadly thin pitch voice as if its the angel of death himself whispering in your ears that he is so envious of your new found ability to fly that he would be taking your soul in return as soon you touch the ground hard enough.

 Sooner I hit the hard rubble ground ending my dreamy fly and land on my feet squatting due to the impact twisting my right ankle and feeling numb on my left leg. I then turn around and see the final and only wall ahead of me needed to climb over to get out of this prison. But the wall seems too tall, almost more than double my height and I already knew it would be this hard to climb over it. I had planned to climb the wall using my feet and crawl on it like the tree climbers or like some Spider man.

 My flexibility made me capable enough to fit and adjust myself through the small gap between the rods of the window space and I trust my abilities enough that I would have managed to climb this wall by crawling on each brick which were somewhat a little protruding outside to the wall which would given me support to put my feet on and climb, but in that plan, having a twisted ankle and a numb leg was not even considered. So here I struggle to even walk towards the wall and then try to lift my one leg high enough to put it on a rusty brick which is a little outside the wall towards me, but that brick too is placed almost till the height of my face, with the excessive pain, the cramps in my leg muscles and the fracture in my ankle it becomes impossible to lift my leg so high upto that height or to even jump high enough to at least hold an another a little outside brick way above the rusty brick and then keep my feet on the rusty one.

'Come on hurry up you fool. How much are you going to pee? You making an Ocean or what?' shouts the guard from outside the toilet. So mission impossible it is with my present state and I know in my mind that sooner than I can expect, the guard waiting for me outside the toilet would come in to check on me and then I would be busted. I keep trying hard to lift my legs or to jump and that in return makes my injuries even more severe and painful. Seconds later I hear a voice

'Wait right there you Bhosdike, trying to run away?' shouts the hawaldaar guard up from the toilet.

It won't be even a minute and the guards would come here and get me, so I take a few steps back and prepare myself to sprint a little to get a start for the jump. I then run with my full speed and jump with all my might as there is another loud crack heard in my right ankle and I hit the brick wall hard in front of me smashing into it like blind bull. I fall on the ground and shout in pain while holding my ankle as the guards come over and get me.

Even though they see that I am in immense pain lying on the ground after hitting the wall and even have the top of my forehead bleeding now, yet they start to bash me down with their baton sticks to show their dominance. Foolish egomaniac oppressors. I pass out.

The following night a doctor is called in the prison and I get treated. He gets up a plaster for my fractures and medicines for my wounds to heal better and faster, from then on life has become much easier in here for me. All part of the day I just have to rest peacefully in my own new private cell where there is even a separate toilet seat in the corner, a guard brings me food and medicines three times a day. Once every week the doctor comes to check up on me and changes my plasters if needed.

The guards are still pretty furious with me and they would definitely have beaten me to pulp after catching me at my failed escape attempt. But my present weak fractured status didn't give them the chance to. One thing is for sure that once I am fully back to my abled body and recovered, they would tie me up in the chains and beat the shit out of me so that not only me but also anybody else doesn't ever get the naturally occuring courageous thought of trying to escape from the prison. Even if someone new later gets the thought, the fear-filled conversations of the other inmates would suppress the thought and desire to even attempt the escape.

Escaping from prison is very much similar to trying to quit smoking; it takes more than just a few attempts. You have to keep trying again and again to leave the prison or the cigarettes and fail, but never give up because eventually one day one time you will succeed in running away from the prison and the tobacco.

It has been two months since my first failed attempt at prison escape and now I am fully back to normal. The doctor just today cuts open my plaster and I am able to walk again comfortably. The very moment the doctor cuts open my plaster, it dawns upon me that from now on there will be no more VIP treatment in the cell for me, I would now lose all the perks such as the separate prison cell with a toilet, guards bringing me food and the sponge baths in the cell. So first I am shifted back to my old cell with the other three inmates who obviously are not that happy, nothing surprising about that. Today is the first day after my injury when again I have to stand with the thin steel plate in the long queue for the food.

God I hate this place, but I will soon think of another idea to get away. I definitely will get out sooner or later. I have to get out.

One early morning the guards wake us up an hour earlier than we normally do. After the bathing and the breakfast, we all prisoners are assembled together in rows of lines and given the task of making arrangements for an acting workshop. Now what the hell is that? Makes me wish more that I had succeeded in my escape attempt earlier.

They say that a very famous Bollywood movie star would be coming from the very next day to teach us drama and theatre acting. To my surprise, except for me, all the other prisoners get pretty excited for it as if he/she is going to feed them milk or something. But I hope they do realize they won't even be touching a hair of that star and that he/she would just be teaching us how to perfect a craft of being fake, which we all are but in different amounts. God people love Drama in their lives, I don't, I just hate drama, I would rather kill my enemy without any drama. The Dramatic death of a target makes it harder for me to forget it and sleep in peace. No place for sentimentality in our line of Business. Only lines of spilled blood.

So the whole day all the prisoners make the arrangements for the workshop as per the guards' orders in the movie hall of our prison. Our movie hall is a big room with lots of seats in front of a large white sheet of screen on which movies as per the guards' choice are played with the help of a projector emitting movies on it which is hung above the seats at the back side of the hall.

I take no part in this movie hall converting task and just stand in the corner of the room with my hands folded as the guards do notice but none say a word, the thing is that even though they do chain me up and beat me brutally sometimes, they all are aware of the fact that I am a deadly assassin who has a kill count of near to 450 and that's what makes fear just too clearly visible in their eyes whenever I see them even when they would be beating me up in the torture room. I sense in their eyes that none of them are foolish enough to make personal enmity with a dreaded killing machine like me.

Raaga too doesn't do any work by himself, instead he is just seating on a folding metal chair and is infact giving detailed instructions to the prisoners around him, his foolish devotees. He is being loud and expressive enough with his exaggerated gestures but not even getting up from the chair.

Hours later, the over enthusiastic prisoners have totally decorated and converted the movie hall into a minimalistic stage of a drama theatre.

The next morning at sharp ten o clock we are all assembled in the make believe drama theatre cum old movie hall of our prison where everyone waits anxiously for the yet unknown to us movie star. Five minutes later, a wonderful strong fragrance of a ladies perfume comes in first as if gates of the paradise just have been slightly opened and then walks in the most beautiful woman in the world. All the prisoners start to clap and hoot on her arrival for the actress Layla Rathod, who comes in with a wide white smile while waving towards us with her long fingers as she comes into the centre of the hall and removes her big brown goggles showing her dark brown eyes. She looks beautifully tan with just a rose lipstick and black lining around her eyes. I always had a crush on her since I saw her in the movies, but seeing her in real life now is just something else. This is the first time when I see her and fall in love with the dark long hair woman with a pointed nose.

To my surprise she isn't wearing any makeup as in movies her face is almost covered with at least three layers of it I feel. Yet she is looking eleven times more attractive even though it is pretty clear that she isn't even trying to look even a bit good here at the moment and is just going as casual as possible. Trying to avoid the wrong kind of attraction I guess.

Love is totally unpredictable and foolishly blinding. No science will ever be able to answer the question that why do we fall in love with someone. It just happens even when you least expect it to. It fucks you up. It is both a curse and blessing on Mankind, this feeling of Love.

I just keep looking at her with awe as everybody else including the guards too, with all the attention at her as she is standing in the center of the hall in between the circle of crowd we have formed around her. A loose black gown with big round silver earrings and her dark hair loosely tied back with just a few long strands coming over her face which maybe done purposefully, with her thin hands coming together as she speaks to us while giving a smile often which shows the dimple at her left cheek. I am just too busy looking at her that I just don't understand a word of her soothing voice and soon the prisoners start to move as if she has given them an instruction. They go towards the stage while five among them go on to the stage with her standing in the middle.

The session ends after an hour as I stand and just keep looking at her from the back end of the crowd without taking any part in the drama or whatever she was trying to teach because honestly speaking there was literally just a romantic music playing in my ears and I didn't hear a word she uttered. I couldn't understand shit.

At night everybody sleeps and I cannot, I just keep thinking about her, was she a woman or just magic? Like either she was a beautiful fragrance or a deadly intoxication? I don't know as for now I just smile wide foolishly while looking at the ceiling wall of the prison cell while falling in the mad deep ocean of love.

Fuck, this is making me crazy and I remember my Boss Karim Lala warning me about women. He would say that you could fuck as many beautiful woman as you like, prostitutes, whores and any wonderful woman you like unless and until you don't catch feelings, pretty woman on bed are great for you, but falling in love is like a deadly disease, to get infected by it is as easy as catching cold but it is even deadlier than any dangerous virus in the world, because it can destroy you and only a very few lucky ones get back the love from the ones they want. More than majority of them are destroyed because of these damn Feelings they catch unexpectedly.

"Always be on guard with your feelings for the woman" he would say. "and the most lethal weapon in the world is not the gun and the bombs, but the beautiful women".

It is said that whatever happens in life, happens for a better reason and is for your own good only. Now my belief in that saying has grown more than just stronger, as until my last killing of the twenty six men, I had already murdered successfully a total of around 450 men and never got caught, but this time unfortunately the cops got me. Now I even have tried to escape and that too failed. So here I am stuck in this shithole prison cursing my luck for until today, now after seeing her it feels like it all happened to be good that I got caught by the cops and even my escape attempt failed as if the universe has conspired all this from the start just so I could meet her in here.

There will be another session day after tomorrow they say and I can't wait for the hours to pass. Every second now feels like pushing a large rock. And I wait for the time to pass and for the next session when I will again get to see her, Layla Rathod, the love of my life, the first and the only woman I fell in love with.

I whisper her name slowly as I lay down and keep saying it until it feels as if my tongue and lips have become familiar and comfortable with the letters of her name. God how beautiful is even is the pronunciation of her name. Fuck I am a gone case.

And I wait.

LAYLA

My alarm goes off and I wake up feeling like shit as always, I smoke a cigarette and have two shots of vodka. After a bath I smoke another and have my black coffee, put on a shabby ill fitted black gown which is my go-to whenever I want to feel comfy and apply just a kaajal eye liner and lipstick, nothing more. No excessive shiny make up, don't want to be getting more than necessary attention of those criminal inmates of the prison. But does this even make sense, they would obviously have all their eyes on me. I then have another shot of vodka and brace myself for my first day first session at the Byculla Prison. Damn! I am seriously doing this. Oddly enough I get the occasional urge to roll a joint and smoke it up, but I realize I don't have it with me and can't even ask Mini now as she would obviously not allow me before going for work and that too at the prison. Smoking weed and going to meet the cops? Such a nonsensical joke it would be, but otherwise too nothing my life is sensical anymore and is a way more than a joke.

She too doesn't keep it with herself anytime and also she is cleaner than a Nun. But whenever I demand it from her to fulfill my cravings even if they are once in a blue moon, as my manager she makes sure to arrange the best and finest quality weed to me. She asks and buys it from trustful friend of hers who has a dealer in contact. But there is no chance of me getting it today or anytime soon until my acting classes at the prison are over, as she would be paranoid about being so near to the cops like literally at their place of shelter. So thump my right fist onto my breast and say it furiously "Fuck this Shit!" to take out my frustration and calm myself down. It takes a while for a star as big as me to getting used to not getting things instantly and the way we want. "Humble" seems like a whole new word.

I meet Mini downstairs near the parking lot waiting for me and as usual sparking with joy and positive energy she hugs me making me feel better, then we get into my white BMW and leave.

I reach on time, just five minutes late, on shoots earlier I used to be even an hour late and nobody would dare to say a word, but here I am today so punctual, just five minutes late than the given time. This is not at all me.

Two hawaldaar guards outside are there to welcome and lead me inside through the courtyard of the prison and there I am shown into a room which they say would be my green room from today onwards. So just outside my green room there is this big front courtyard of the prison.

Standing here at the dark olive colored door of my newly given prep room, I can see the black rods of the main gate of the prison and my white BMW just behind it shining like a star under the sun.

Inside my room for now as I and Mini take a tour, there is just a big oval mirror on a table which is like a dresser of the cheapest kind it looks but yet the mirror has got glittering golden color at the frame edge with sharp artistic textures, a leather covered metal chair in front of it and a lightweight plastic chair behind the metal chair including a big ceiling fan and a long light bulb are the only furniture of this so called prep green room of mine. I at once instruct Mini to get the dresser table filled up by some of my make up and touch up essentials as I say her goodbye again. She doesn't fail to sense that I am of course not that happy with this job. Everybody dreads changes. I take a deep breath and prepare myself mentally. Brace myself for whatever it is about to come next and walk towards the door realizing that no matter how many friends, colleagues and lovers a person could have, but when you are in deep shit, you got only you yourself. You yourself are the one and only truest and most loyal friend of your ownself.

Dwelling upon it as I reach outside, just a little walk to the left from the door of my this room and another left that takes me through a dark brick walled passageway of this prison which feels like this phase of my own life until I see a bright light at the end of it which is of the big hall where already lots of inmates there are waiting eagerly for me which is evident from the overenthusiastic clapping and whistling of theirs to welcome me. I hope so badly that even my life would replicate the cheerfulness and brightness of this hall at the end of the dark passageway. I stand in the centre of the room and start to speak as all the eyes of the prisoners around me forming a circle stay glued on me, that's when I see him.

There are two types of men, One who are sweet enough to lend me the shoulder to cry on, these are the ones who want to fuck me. The Second are the rude ones who cause the sadness in me making me cry and don't care about my feelings anymore; these are the ones who have already fucked me.

But today I just found a new kind of a man. The one about whom I have not been able to comprehend yet, the way he is looking at me is neither of the two types. There is just something else in his eyes rather than just lust and love, something way more than this worldly things, maybe it is just some other kind of love in his eyes which I hadn't come across until now. A love from another world or maybe from some another place not known to foolish man yet.

There is definitely something different about the way he is looking at me even though there are around fifty prisoners along with him looking at me at the moment. But he is different, his eyes are conveying something else.

He just stands at the back and keep looking at me with those hallucinating unique eyes while not taking part in any of the activities we do for the day.

After the session ends I come back to my home and have a smoke and open up a new bottle of whisky, then go off to bed, I anyway don't have anything else to do for now. Being awake and sober for longer periods makes me feel suicidally depressed and sad again, brings back all the negative memories and the heartbreaks back, so it's better to not be sober and awake for long and just go off to bed intoxicated. Past haunts like the Greatest Demon.

I lie on my bed and see a text message from Mini

"Hope everything went alright today?"

I don't reply, not that I don't want to reply but I don't have the energy now to and I am pretty sure she will understand that. She always understands. I doze off to sleep and I dream those eyes of his.

Fuck! these men.

CHARLES

Finally! Today is the day of our second session, how hard it had been to go through yesterday as I waited so eagerly for today. Today will be the second time I will get to see her and today I plan to make an impression, a very good one. Last time she wouldn't have even seen my face for sure yet alone know about my existence, but today I will at least make her aware of myself. Just yesterday I went to the guy who washes and irons our prison uniforms, asked him with utmost politeness to iron mine a little more than usual to make my clothes crispier, of course he obeyed but at first he was bedazzled at my approach since until yesterday I had never spoken to him or anyone in the prison in that case. He wasn't expecting that kind of politeness and it's very rare even for me to show this soft side of mine. Somewhere a little soft part of the heart of the Devil.

Luckily yesterday was the weekly shaving and hair cutting day at the prison, where the prisoners who know the "Art of the Barber" do the job in the courtyard where stool chairs are placed on the ground and a small mirror is given to hold in the hand of the guy sitting on the stool for his haircut and shave. There are three barbers which makes it three lines of us prisoners behind them waiting for their turn. I didn't stand in the barber line and didn't do a haircut or a shave since I have arrived here, but yesterday I did. So many first times I have been having recently. First time in a prison, first time trying to escape in the prison, first failure at the prison escaping attempt, first time talking to any prisoner inside and the first time falling in love with a women head over heels.

Every single person in their heads think of themselves as the most perfect and beautiful human being, but I on the other hand am totally aware of the fact that I just look average, not that great looking and not even that bad looking, just average or maybe a bit above average. Layla Rathod is the top actress in Bollywood, loved and wanted by many and she looks so gorgeous that it feels to an average looking man like me, that getting her would just be a dream as she actually seems to be way out of my league. She has got killer looks while I am just a killer.

So getting my clothes ironed better, a shave and a haircut seems like my only option while even considering the pretty limited resources in the prison for a man to look good and well groomed.

LAYLA

My sleep gets disturbed because of Mini's call, I pick it up in an almost sleepy state while trying to keep my eyes as closed as possible to not lose that sweet deep state of sleepiness and then she makes me aware that today is another session day for teaching drama at the Prison. Aah Fuck.

I get up as usual with the help of a cigarette and black coffee, and then put on blue skinny jeans and a loose white kurti over it. Today too I reach on time and as the previous time the prisoners are all already ready waiting for me in the theatre hall welcoming me again with a big round of applause.

I go up on to the stage and today I do have an idea, I first ask them all to get seated on the seats in front of the stage as I start talking. I give them a few basic tips about acting which I am not sure whether they understand or not, so to apply it I even try to make them do a scene with me.

First I call upon the stage a fellow prisoner with me and do a scene where two new lovers are just sharing their deep feelings for the first time with each other. I hold the prisoner's rough hands in mine and explain to him what we shall be doing which most probably he doesn't get it which is evident from his plainest expression as if I am speaking some rocket science to him. The thing about acting it is said, that it cannot be thought, Only a person who wants to become an actor, loves the art of acting and at least tries somewhat to act can be the only one who can understand what you say to him regarding the art and can transfer atleast a bit of your knowledge into him, even the slightest will to genuinely try to act would be enough for me to work on a person, but here these prisoners don't seem that passionate about acting, this is just another fun activity for them. So I recollect my thoughts that I just need to do my job and don't feel bothered about them not learning, because at the end of the day all that matters for them is that these acting sessions should be fun and games, because obviously none of them even if they get out of prison would go for acting auditions and try to become an actor.

I look in the prisoner's cold swollen eyes and say my dialogue of love and then there is a silence from his side as he looks at me blankly until I instruct him what he should be saying and he repeats the same dialogue after me word to word lifelessly as if we are doing a scene where his mother has died and not a romantic one.

Soon I call upon more prisoners to do the scene with me one by one and all of them don't fail to disappointment me.

 Now it feels that these prisoners are only coming up on the stage just so that they can get the chance to hold my hands because they are not even trying to act even when I am giving them such good detailed instructions. The effort I am putting in to teach, even an infant would be able to do it. God knows I am trying. If there ever would have been a law for restricting the worst actors from acting then this prisoners here for sure would have even got life imprisonment punishment for that.

 After doing the lifeless act with fourteen prisoners on the stage it then starts to feel really tiring. I could do twenty eight takes and still have the bone and enthusiasm to do ten more on our movie sets with my professional co-stars which sometimes are even better actors than me and that is becuase of the dedication every single person and the crew shows on the set, it is the perfect environment to live the life of our acting parts even though it all looks total chaos from far. Here nobody is giving a damn about my sacred art of acting, so carefree and ignorant these people are, but the ones watching from their seats are all having a good time and a laugh. They keep laughing louder and clapping on seeing their fellow inmates act weirdly on the stage with me. Then when I feel I had it enough, I shout loudly at them

'Is there anyone among you who would seriously do the act? This is not funny, come on. Anyone who would at least try to do it properly?'

Then there is complete silence among them, none is laughing or clapping anymore, just confused wide eyes of theirs fixed on me. They were not at all expecting such furiosness from me, they would think of me as just a beautiful actress to look at and praise the Creator for his Creation. So I tone down my voice and a little politely I speak again remembering that for these foolish people I might just be an eye candy.

'I know you guys are not actors, none of you have even acted ever before, But at least when you come up here, I want you to try to do your part truthfully and honestly. This is not a circus or a funny talk show where we need to make the ones watching laugh. You get my point. So from now on, whoever I call or comes here on the stage, I want you to do your part sincerely and give your best okay? So who will come now?' I ask and for a while there is no response from them, they just continue with the mindless staring as if I just spoke in French. Then there at the very back of the crowd of the seated prisoners, A hand is slowly raised in the air. I look at it and then call

'Okay good, come on.'

The man who had just raised his hand gets up and it turns out to be the same guy who was looking at me with his hallucinating eyes last time. As he walks while still looking at me without blinking, I for sure can notice that today he has got his hair and beard trimmed and that his white uniform with the black stripes looks a bit over ironed and too straightly crisp creases as if just another touch of the hot iron and the cloth would have burned. The heads of the prisoners turn to look at who that is and their gaze follows him throughout as he finally reaches up on the stage near me. He comes and grasps my hands into his warmer ones and keeps looking into my eyes without breaking eye contact with a slight smirk on his face as if he knows every single thing about the Worlds and the Universe. There is something strong about his eyes, I can feel it. I keep looking into them and I realize that he is waiting for me to speak out the dialogues which I have done so many times with so many prisoners today until now, but who knew that this was going to be different. I quickly get into my character and start

'I wanted to say something'

'I too wanted to say something' he answers quickly in his deep baritone

'What?' I ask

'No you said before, so you tell me first, what you wanted to say?' he asks

'Well I..uh..I really think we are good friends and that' he starts to softly rub the tips of his thumbs over the skin of my hands as I pause

'and what?' he asks

I look down now breaking the eye contact as he continues to look at my face, for the first time in a while I start to blush, then I look back into his eyes which now seems difficult to. To be looking into his ocean like eyes and still being in my character while not getting lost in them and distracted from here is getting almost impossible for me. Yet I continue as he gives just a casual yet confident smile as if he is being able to intrepret the chaos going on in my mind at the very moment. As if every thought in my mind is being magically fabricated by he himself.

'I really like the connection we both have and the understanding between each other, I am the most Alive when I am with you, I feel we can be more than just friends maybe?' I say my lines and wait for his dialogue

'You won't believe that but I too was going to say the same thing, that I have started to fear Death only after I met you, what a coincidence!' he says the same dialogue which I have been instructing the other prisoners until now to say, but the way he says it totally feels as if he has been an actor all his life and the character he is playing is he himself and even the prisoners don't laugh or clap because they are helplessly being pulled into this magic of a scene on the stage. That's what happens when actors actually play their part with the truthfulness from the deepest of their souls and heart, the audience unknowingly falls in love with them. So

I am astonished because either this guy in front of me is a seasoned actor with some serious skills or he is just being himself and has totally fallen for me. I don't know which part among the two is more horrible. There is utter silence as I continue to say my line but then he interrupts me

'There is a moon and the stars and I have seen men promising it to the love of their life to bring it for them. Now I don't know if anyone has tried that actually or would do it any day, but when I see in the sky I can still see the moon and the stars which makes me realize that no one has been able to bring that for their love until now. So an average guy like me cannot promise you the moon and the stars to prove my indefinite love for you, but all I can say is that I love you and will do so until there is life in me, I will be with you forever, whenever you need me and will give you whatever I can because in this world all I have is my own heart of river, whose sweetest water I would want to empty in the sea of love, That love of my heart is the only thing I can promise to you.' he says the whole thing with his eyes fixed into mine as if they see the whole of my world through it. I blush and get totally hallucinated in him and for the moment I totally forget that what he has just said was not the part of the script. Before I can get back into my reality and do something, he leans forward to kiss me, his lips touch mine and makes me feel like something which I have never ever touched, the feeling is indescribable as his hands slowly slid over to my hips and we kiss. The sense of time and reality all seem to be lost in that very moment, for now I don't even know who he is and as we keep kissing and running our tongues into each other, I don't even care about who he is or why he is here because for now he makes me feel like I never ever been made to feel.

I am Lost in Him.

We spend a lifetime or maybe an eternity in that kiss until the loud clapping and shouting of the overenthusiastic prisoners seated make me come back to my present reality as I let go off his heavenly lips and take a step back. He opens his eyes slowly then and gives me a beautiful smile as if just read my mind once again. I am red and still blushing more for sure as I turn quickly to face the audience of prisoners seated in front of me and try to speak, but I stumble and find my voice breaking. I try not to look back into his eyes because I know that I will totally loose it and not at all be in my control if I look back into his hallucinating ocean eyes. I take a deep breath and then speak

'That's what you call good acting; give another round of applause for him guys.' I say and they again clap as I pat his bicep without looking at him. For sure he has got his gaze fixed at me even now as he keeps looking at me admiringly and goes off the stage back to his seat at the very back.

I guess and hope that these prisoners didn't understand that what happened on the stage was not a part of the play we were doing and all just happened actually in the moment. Damn, even though I loved the way he kissed me, it seriously was not at all a good idea. I maybe should have just pulled myself back instantly, but I know I couldn't have. There is definitely something about his eyes, the way he looks at me. I lose and find myself in him.

CHARLES

Another sleepless night for me, as I again lay down and keep looking at the plaster tearing of the ceiling of my prison cell, busy in my beautiful thoughts. It is total darkness in here and just a few rays of bright soothing light of the white moon coming in through the thin small rectangular gap high up on the wall of this prison cell which is there for ventilation. There is a loud snore of a fellow inmate who does that every time he sleeps, but that doesn't bother me, I in fact now like it. That's the thing that when in love you even start to like the things which you hated before.

It's going to be a long night since I know I am going to be awake through the most of it, just thinking about her, thinking about today. All these fools got the chance to go up on the stage and do the act with her. The golden chance to act out a romantic scene with the most beautiful woman on the planet ever and all of them messed it up so foolishly even embarrassing her.

I wasn't expecting even the least for Raaga himself to go on to the stage to take part in that acting, I thought he would be totally uninterested in this type of creative art and he proved me right when after going there he too was just buffooning around like all the others before him. But honestly I was only really concerned when he was with her on the stage. The way he was looking at her made me feel quite uneasy. I don't know, maybe it was just the sheer brutal coldness of his evil eyes being casted upon her from so close as standing next to her, that was what giving me those bad vibes.

 I never had any passion for acting and I know I never will be able to do any of it, in this life all I can do is to Kill. To kill people is my only ability. So when I went on the stage today to do the act with her, I knew that if I tried to act then I too like the prisoners before me on the stage would have messed it all up and made it all look like a complete joke. That would obviously gotten her more embarrassed and surely left a bad impression and uninterested in me. It's all about making those right impressions on the person you like. I don't even remember where and when I read this. But yeah I do have a good memory, like I do remember old long boring stuff I might have seen in a movie or read somewhere.

 So today all I did on that stage was to be my true self without even trying to fake it and poured out all the heavy load of feelings of my foolish heart which I actually felt for her. I was not acting at all, I was just being me. Whatever I said and did on the stage was the truth of my soul and I am pretty much sure that she did sense it. I was expecting her to move back when I went in to kiss her, but she did not. If she wanted she would have even slapped me at the moment and made a scene. Could have gotten offended and scolded me, then even the guards would have straightened me out for a good couple of days in the torture cell, but she didn't. I took my chances and thank god, it worked. One thing life has taught me is that if I don't take my chances then obviously I will fail. But if I do then there is a chance I might succeed. And today I succeeded. I honestly felt she lovingly enjoyed that wonderful moment we had. Even after the kiss she was blushing in a joyous mood though not looking towards me after that for the day.

No one among the prisoners and the guards was clever enough to realize that what we did on the stage was not a part of the act, but I was actually doing what my heart wanted to do. Just following my instincts. Definitely they would have been even then so jealous watching me kissing her so passionately.

Karim Lala Bhai would often teach me the utmost importance of following our gut, when he would invite me to his home for a dinner of deliciously cooked Mutton Biryani, while feasting on it he would try to explain the significance of it, that our gut feeling and intuition is a totally unique part of us, sacred and mysterious as he would like to believe that it is the Universe or the Creator or a Power higher than us communicating in this way. Learning to listen to it and respecting it is the greatest way to move forward in life, and at the end of the day we are all slaves to our heart, we do what it makes us do. So I guess her not moving back is a sign that her heart too has got a good liking towards me? Maybe? Maybe not? I don't care, I will try my chances again at her in the next session, but God that is after a gap of four days now. How bad I wish there were more than just two sessions of her drama class in a week. Damn! Thinking about Karim Bhai now has made me crave the Mutton Biryani and Kheer Desert after it. I can almost remember and feel the taste of them in my mouth.

For now all I have is my thoughts, mostly about her and the time to get through. I am so glad I didn't succeed in my attempt to escape the prison that day, because if I would have, then I would have never found her. Now I have different plans, I won't run way from this prison until she keeps teaching her sessions here. At least until then I am here. I decide to listen to my heart this time. For Intuition. For Love.

LAYLA

M ini walks into the bedroom and wakes me up. Yeah, she has her own set of keys to my apartment. I gave them to her when we both realized years ago that the only way I would waking up on time for the shoots would be with the help of her physically waking the drunk wasted me up from my bed and attacking me with a cold shower. No wonder she is more and an assistant and like a sister to me. Even more than that I guess. It not at all makes me proud accepting that she did had to wake me up from my drunk sleep way too many times than just a few occasions. So the decision of giving her a seperate set of keys was definitely good one.

Today I am not even that drunk, but somedays she just likes to be there to wake me up. She didn't even try calling today. Somedays when she would get in the house early morning without any warning and then see a man lying naked next to me on my bed, she would just close back the door to my bedroon and sit patiently having breakfast on the living room couch until the Man would leave.

So today she again make me coffee and we sit in the same couch as always when she asks

'So how are your classes at the prison going on?'

'Well can't complain, they are just fine' I reply casually while deciding not to tell her about the kiss with a stranger prisoner and the fact that I actually liked it.

But Mini senses maybe from my expression that I am hiding something from her

'That's it? Nothing more you want to say about it?'

'Nah, it's just okay.' I shrug

She nods and looks away at the windows into the endless clear skies..

The thing is that since that day at the prison, I feel much lighter and less depressed. I do drink and smoke, but way less than before and not with the sole intention of just killing myself quickly. I have done intimate scene with the actors before in the movies and have even kissed and went to bed with a men too many, but the kiss with that stranger in the prison that day was different. Nothing like all the other men I have tasted before. Many have touched me, but his few touches not only made me feel loved after a long time but also like never before. His warm fingertips on my flesh felt like the touch of Paradise.

* * *

Today is the third day of our drama classes at the prison, I get up by myself and five minutes after that my alarm goes off surprising myself. Rarer than the blue moon itself that I am awake before my alarm. I don't feel like drinking or smoking still I just smoke one and have the usual black coffee. It's been a while since I felt even a little good as I am doing today. Not that things have started to become great for me, but just I feel a kind of an excitement for going to the prison for taking the acting classes. I stand in my balcony which is the 24th floor of this wonderful posh building right in the middle of Bombay. Everyone who stays here in this building and in the nearby area knows that they have made it in life, as the cost of living here is just too high for any average person to afford. I enjoy the breeze touching on my face and it makes me realize that how long I haven't come here in this blissful balcony of mine as before I used to come here often to have a relaxing smoke with such a breathtaking view. Up here there is always an almost inaudible sound of the subtle wind which is melodiously calming and soothing as if the angels themselves are whispering to each other. Tiny cars and tiny people, making me realize that I am still on the top even without any good work in my hands. I will definitely make it again in life.

After a shower, I feel like to dress up good and put on a lot of makeup after a long time. It takes half an hour in front of my mirror sitting on the dresser and then I leave quickly without any more delay after seeing the time on my phone as I would love to keep my newly found habit of punctuality.

Does Love actually Change You ?

CHARLES

After four long tiring and the slowest days of my life ever, finally is the day for the next drama class of ours, another day when I will get to see her - My Princess, My Beauty, My Love. So she comes in today looking all dolled up. She is wearing black leggings and a body fit black t shirt showing her generous curves. All in black like the Devil except she was looking like an Angel. Her face today looks much brighter and glossier as if she has spent a lot of time doing the actress makeup. Or maybe she has directly come here after a night shoot. But she doesn't look tired enough for that. Today she doesn't look like the depressedly hurt and wasted Layla Rathod with whom I fell in love in the earlier classes, but the movie star Layla Rathod in her element. As usual she starts the session standing in the middle of the crowd formed by us as I can observe that the prisoners today are looking more at her body than her eyes as she talks.

She tries teaching us some more basics about the art of acting which none of us as usual understand shit, as the whole time until then she avoids an eye contact with me. Her lips look fuller and shinier, a lip gloss for sure, there is something pink colored above her eye lids and very little something red applied on her cheeks. She keeps talking to the crowd with the beautiful gesture of her thin slender hands and long fingers on which there is a very thin like wire golden ring on one of them. Damn she has got her nail cut and no exotic nail polish. The attractive expressions of the widening of her eyes and breaking into a casual smile often that show her big rabbit like white teeth which would have looked ugly on someone else, but on her they seem to perfectly compliment her overall thick lips and the smooth rounded structure of her jaw. Her that smile is making me fall in love even with this Movie Star version of Layla Rathod. Once done with her teaching, she then divides the fifty of us into five groups of ten men each and gives us all groups a task of making up a play act. Group task to us fools? Is she a bigger fool?

 For sure none will be able to make a good play, like what is she even expecting giving the stupid prisoners a task of preparing up a whole play all by themselves from scratch. Was their display of their superbly talented acting skills on the stage with her last time not enough for her to realize how dumb they actually are as actors? They don't even have the C of Creativity inside their heads, which mostly would be full of shit. Maybe she does fully understand that and is just trying to do her job.

 As the five groups stand separate from each other

and start to discuss the play they will be doing in the later upcoming sessions, she goes a little away from the entire crowd and stands near a dusty table at the entrance of the hall and starts looking at her cell phone. I observe that and just take a few steps away from my group as they anyway are not that much interested to include me in the play, none are my friends here. They keep talking to each other with so much enthusiasm and energy in their voices and eyes as if they are going to prepare a play worthy enough to win an Oscar, that is if there is an Oscar for the plays too. But I already know that they will not be able to prepare anything. My gut says that even Layla knew that they wouldn't be able to do shit and gave the task purposefully so that she can get a break to just stand aside quietly, maybe just maybe waiting and giving Me a chance to approach?

So I start taking slow steps in her direction as none from my team even gets bothered from my absence.

I keep taking my steps towards her and I can again feel my heart pumping faster and the very same feeling of notorious butterflies in my stomach as the previous time when I walked up on to the stage to her. Whenever I am walking towards her, I instantly feel as if taking a stroll in an other wordly garden. I finally reach near the dusty table without my heart popping out of my chest and stand next to her right arm as she keeps looking down at her cell phone and acts as if she hasn't noticed my arrival yet and then I slowly keep my elbows on the table in front of us and lean over while looking up left at the most beautiful face of hers. She then looks up from the phone at me with her round eyes and for a moment I feel vulnerable, A killer I am and the people with me usually are the ones who feel vulnerable and scared for their lives, but now here for the first time it was the other way round. We keep looking at each other blankly for a while buried deep in each other's eyes and then to avoid any awkwardness I realize I will have to speak to break this poetic silence even though I feel my eyes just now had said enough already

'Hey'

'Hi' she answers cheerfully and breaking into a casual smirk as she further asks

'Shouldn't you be there with your group right now, preparing for the play?'

I look down on the dust at the table and then look again at her to speak

'I should, but I had a question in my mind which I really needed to ask you eagerly'

'Do you? So what do you want to ask?'

'In the last session when I came on the stage to act with you, did you realize that what all I said and did up there was not an act and was all the truth of my heart?' I say and now my heart almost feels like it has come up to my throat

Now she looks down on the table with genuine shyness or maybe that's just acting while putting back the long strands of hair falling on her face behind her left ear and answers

'Was it?'

'Umm...yeah. It was' I say, then she again looks back into my eyes and replies

'I have been an actor for many years now, acting is not only my passion but now it has even become a part of me and my identity, so with enough experience as an actress, I clearly can feel and make out the difference when a person is acting and not.' she says and then keeps looking in to my eyes blushing as she almost breaks into a wide smile and so do I, my gaze then goes towards her thick glossy pink lips and for the moment I feel like to just kiss and squeeze them with my lips and float away in the madness of love. But I don't, I control myself thinking about the surrounding prisoners and the guards. I don't care about myself, but a person of her stature kissing a nobody like me would cause a lot of problems for her surely. I am just busy in my thoughts while still looking at her beautiful luscious lips subconsciously and controlling the uncontrollable urge to grasp her in my arms and kiss her till the end of the world, but instantly she leans a little lower while bringing her pretty face near to mine and before I can even realize, the lips of the Goddess has touched mine.

I instantly feel as if we have just been transported to an another world, a world where the sky isn't blue but just purple with too many red stars shining ferociously announcing my new found love, a world where only she and me exist, a world where I am not a prisoner of a fucked up jail in Bombay, but a prisoner to her Sacred Love, where I don't have to kill for a living but only make endless Love to her the whole day, where every single day I get to explore every single inch of her precious body. I'm her's and she's mine, together all we do is madly make the love of our passions as if that's the sole purpose for the Universe to exist all this time. In my own thoughts and the world of my own in my mind with my eyes closed and I can still feel the softest lips and the wet tongue of hers in my mouth and that's when I just unfortunately come back to my reality and open my eyes, her eyes are yet closed.

An eternity in a moment, but soon she too comes back to her senses and becomes conscious of our surrounding as she instantly pulls her face back. As she then opens her round eyes, I can see myself in the iris of her dark eyes as if I am drowning in them and only She can save me.

We both look at each other for a while until she

breaks the eye contact and looks at her side towards the crowd of the prisoners. Then we see a chubby short heighted prisoner with really short hair and little beard without any moustache looking at us with wide eyes. With his gaze fixed on us without any blinking as if like a zombie he starts to walk towards us and I know that he mostly won't have any good intentions for her after seeing us kissing like that. The jail makes any good man a sexually frustrated monster and we all here are savages after all, as he keeps coming near towards us, I take a step forward and pull her softly with the utmost care behind me, standing in front of her with my back facing her like a mountain there to protect her from any beast of evil. Damn he is going to cause a disastrous scene, that's my nervous prediction. He keeps on approaching and soon he walks up to a little away to our right and I get myself prepared to knock the fuck out of him, but soon we both realize that the prisoner is not even looking at us and keeps on with his walking as he passes though us from the right side and goes behind us. So he was looking at the guards way beyond us at the entrance and was going there. He continues his walking uninterrupted and reaches to the guards far behind us as we take a sigh of relief. He asks the guards something and then one of them goes away with him, maybe he needed to go to the loo. I then turn around fully and can see the immense tension on her face and the sweat on her forehead as we both break into the widest grin looking at each other.

I always thought that luck was never on my side, but I guess all the luck of my life was being saved so that it could be used today altogether, all of the luck just to make me lucky for this moment as none of the prisoners have looked at us kissing. They all are still busy deeply in their conversations and preparations of a play like some little school children to whom the teacher has given a group project and all of them are just having a good time talking to each other in the team. I then look at all the guards at the corners of this large room and luckily again none of them too has seen us kissing so passionately right in front of so many people. The guards too seem to be engaged in their own conversations with each other. A miracle like this happening feels almost like an impossibility which I can't believe but just be thankful for that it did just happen.

Only with the help of the Universe can miracles happen.

My luck and maybe the God which they say exists was on my side today. Only today. We then look at each other again and grin foolishly as she again looks back into her mobile phone and I take a few steps back to go stand just near my group. We have a play to prepare.

LAYLA

I did that purposefully of course, gave all the prisoners a group task so that they could just be busy with themselves and I could stand away in peace from all of them. That way I knew I would be giving Him the chance to come talk to me and thank god he did. He walked to me and just stood there, every step he took towards me made my pulse go faster as if a vein would explode before he would reach until me.

He stood beside me and started to talk making me mesmerized with his deep baritone voice, I at first tried to avoid looking into his eyes as I knew that if as before I do, then I would lose myself again in that deep ocean like hallucinating eyes. I definitely will ask him next time whether if he actually tries to do something on me with his eyes, is that some sort of black magic or an evil art of hypnosis or seduction he has learned somewhere or maybe it's just that he looks at me the way nobody else does and that's what does the magic on me?

He asked me a question and I subconsciously looked at him and there I made the first mistake. Instant regret as I kept speaking to him as we talked further and then suddenly he stopped while just innocently looking at my lips. I knew he wanted to kiss me and I did too, it was heavenly the last time we did, but I also knew with all the rumors and news about me going on and so many people around me, kissing him would mean saying a goodbye to my career, that is if it later comes out in the news, so obviously an actress as popular as me even if she had the slightest sense in her brains then she would have never done something so foolish like kissing a stranger prisoner in front of fifty other criminals and at least eight police guards. But I lost my mind when I met his gaze, those eyes of an angel who would make anyone do anything without questions, I had lost myself and was nowhere in my control anymore, and before I could even realize where in the world had I gone lost, I had darkness in front of my eyes as they were closed and my tongue was juggling in his mouth. Gosh! I should have been a little easier with the tongue, it could have freaked him out. Showing my kinkiness too soon. I pulled myself back as soon as I remembered about the people around me and then looked around, to my surprise none there was looking at me or us, seemed as if no one saw us making love right there.

That one foolish prisoner who was looking at me blankly and walking towards us freaked the hell out of me, felt as if he had been seeing us the whole time, but it turns out he was just going to the guards standing far behind us. Luckily none of the guards saw us doing that practically stupid yet the most ethereal kiss of love. But the thing that has stayed with me and touched me deep is the way he pushed me behind him and stood in front of me like a guardian angel. That was the sweetest thing any man has ever done for me. What if that guy was actually walking towards us and would have tried to lay a hand on me and then for sure my stranger lover would have beaten him up, but that only would have made the guards maybe furious and they too would have started to attack us, then my lover would have had to fight all of them and then maybe even the guards would have joined against us. So my stranger lover didn't care about anything at that moment and just stepped forward to cover me from anything that would have come our way. But thank God nothing came our way though. Stuff like that uplifts my soul and somewhat once again instills my belief in the fucked up humanity. Or maybe here it was just the Foolish Love that was making him do that.

I come back home today and I see myself glowing as I look in the mirror. I hadn't seen my skin glowing like this for a long time, not only my skin but my whole body feels as if just been resurrected. Depression had made me dull and suicidal. I still do smoke cigarettes but I don't feel like drinking anymore. Now I don't feel like killing myself and just ending all this, instead now I feel like living, all because of that stranger prisoner lover of mine about whom I yet don't know anything. At night I cannot sleep, it's not just because I am not drinking my alcohol but because I cannot stop thinking about him. He seems like a fantasy, a fantasy that just doesn't seem real. I know that even if I fall asleep, I will have dreams of him. Later I go into my balcony and its dark outside. Just two or three stars twinkling in the dark sky with a nail like moon. I light up and see the grey smoke of my cigarette go off slowly making artistic designs into the dark open air. From this high up in the balcony I can see just the street lights and a few vehicles moving. No sight of wake humans this late into the night. A distance far away when I shorten my eyes forcing them to look more than their limit, I can see people sleeping on the edge of the footpaths. Pushing ourselves will often lead us to new discoveries.

CHARLES

Will she ever be mine? Like totally just mine and nobody else's in the world ever? Every inch of her mine forever ? Can that happen? I don't know and I can't even think the other way, scares me too bad. Day after tomorrow we meet again and today I don't even realize but after a long time I fall asleep and dream of her. All the other nights until tonight I would just be awake the whole time and deeply keep thinking about her, loving every second of it. The one thing I love the most about her is that small black dot on her right cheek near to her nose. In the movies that birthmark like dot is not visible on her face, maybe the makeup team hides it to make her look Perfect, but for me that black dot even makes her look more than just Perfect. Is that what you call a beauty dot? Perfection among Imperfections is what pleases the eye of the lovers. But what do those movie fools know?

Next night again I get into the comfiest sleep.. These last two days I think, think and just think about her while smiling foolishly looking at the ceiling of my prison cell and then without realizing I fall asleep like a baby.

A red beautiful dress, sleeveless it is and a little

above her knees, I don't know what it is called, I never in my life had the need to know about it, she looks angelic enough in that with those round curves of her in that tight dress, she has got long black heels and is sitting on a high stool next to me in a bar sipping red wine. She has got bright red lipstick and there is so much excitement in her eyes as she meets mine while still sipping through her glass. Then she smiles and I feel dead cold in the moment. The upper teeth of her even though a little bigger than normal like the cutest rabbit, are in a perfect alignment as if she had put on braces back when she was a child or maybe after becoming an actress she got them done and whitened by a doctor or maybe she always had such perfect upper teeth, but the bottom teeth of hers are totally out of order. Some are a little front while some are a little back, none are at a place where they should be and all are almost in different sizes, so that is why she smiles in the movies with just her lips closed, but this imperfectness among her bottom teeth turns me on. She has got a little makeup on, but still that black dot on her cheek is still clearly visible. I guess I have already told her how much I love that black little dot and that's why she doesn't feel the need to conceal it.

I have already finished my glass of wine and would want to order another one to the bartender on the other side of this long bar table we are seated at. But before that I feel the strong urge to do something else, I grab her hand and kiss her at the back of her palm, then go on kissing on the smoothest skin of her forearm as I keep kissing and moving up on her whole arm until her shoulder and then I kiss her on the side of her neck. I don't know why but I feel like to bite her neck and I do as she shivers while catching the hair on the back of my head with force, my teeth almost pierced into the delicate flesh of her neck makes me feel alive and reborn as I go on kissing further through the bottom of her chiseled jaw line and then her chin. I again bite her chin as she moans and drops the glass of red wine on the floor as it breaks into a shiny million pieces. I then kiss a little on her lips and then go for her pointed nose. I lick it before kissing that one small black dot on her right cheek. God knows how much I appreciate that black dot on hers. Now I am sure that's why dots like that on the skin are called beauty marks.

I then come back to her lips and just let my feelings take control of myself as I bite the lower lip of her and taste the little blood out of it on my restless tongue. She then suddenly pushes me away as I land back on my stool. She then gets up from her stool, climbs on me and starts to kiss me while unbuttoning my shirt. That's when I feel that all the people in the club and the bartenders have just disappeared or maybe they are right there where they were but the lights around us have all gone dark and she and I are the only ones who are still visibly glowing in the dark as even the music goes louder. And soon the music changes its tune while growing more painfully louder. So loud as if the music is pissed, angry and shouting at me as she intensely keeps bouncing on me and soon I open my eyes to see a hawaldaar guard forcing me to get up while striking his baton stick hard on the metal rods of my cell gate where the three prisoners who are locked up with me are nowhere to be seen now. So they have already gotten up and left to the toilet whereas I got left behind since I was busy in my Beautiful Dream. I soon realise that we are again waken up an hour earlier than the normal even though we don't have any session today or until the next two days for that fact. Until today we were waken up an hour earlier only on the two particular days of the week when there used to be our drama classes. Something seems fishy today then, as usual we all are first allowed in the large men's bathroom but today we aren't allowed to shower as we normally do, instead the guards say that we all would have the bath later and then after that we stand in the long queue for our breakfast in the prison canteen.

It's then that everyone is brought to the open courtyard near the entrance of our jail and there I see a circle lined formed across the edges with the help of small bags of mud, this looks like a mini playground right in between the courtyard.

That's when two guys walk in between and everyone else forms a circle around this make believe playground as crowd. So the two heavy guys in the centre of the ring shake their hands and then a hawaldaar guard whistles.

Turns out today was the day decided for the annual wrestling match in the prison. No one talks to me, so no wonder I didn't get any news about this event.

The two big guys start to fight and quickly a winner is made after he lifts and smacks down the opponent on his face. The loser lies on the ground unconscious. The winner is the prison celebrity 'RAAGA' who keeps his hands up in the air as the other prisoners who already were a big fan of him cheer and clap. Soon the body of the unconscious loser is dragged away and a hawaldaar guard pushes in another opponent in the ring big enough to face the mighty Raaga.

He tries to give Raaga a tough competition, but soon he too is knocked out hard on the ground. They all know how to fight, but not that proper and efficiently. Their skill isn't impeccable. The crowd of prisoners now not only cheer and clap for him as he demands while standing tall in the ring under the bright sun, but they now also start chanting his name. Next two opponents together are pushed in who are a little shorter than Raaga. They too try to give him a fight while working as a team against him, but of course they too fail miserably as he throws each of them far away after hitting them mercilessly, almost killing them. The crowd is now in total awe and pleased for the Mighty Raaga, but not me. For me he just seems to be the King with One eye among the Blind. So then when no one else is yet remaining or willing to get in the ring with this merciless killing machine as he just waits for a while and is about to leave declared as a clear undefeated Champion of this Tournament, I step into the RING.

 I'm just 5.7' with a slim muscular body and Raaga seems at least more than 6.3' with a great body mass. So he looks way bigger than me and everyone else including Raaga himself underestimates me. I wouldn't blame him, comparing the difference between our both sizes would make anyone do that mistake. And that's the first mistake Raaga makes, underestimating me by arrogantly laughing upon me and then looking at me as if I am his innocent prey which he would he eat up raw while the crowd of prisoners join him in the loud mockery laugh. I pay no heed, I am confident, I always am. Not on my body or size, but on my abilities. Raaga might be a good fighter, a huge strong one, maybe even a professionally trained one, and looks like even his crowd knows that, maybe that is why they respect him so much like a King, out of fear, but not a single soul among the foolishly scared crowd of prisoners know that I on the other hand am a professional killer, so professional that I am the one you hire to kill the number one professional killer. As long as I remember the only thing I know is to Kill, that's the only thing I know to do properly and Perfectly, And I love every bit of my killing job. So for me right now here in this prison wrestling competition which is just a friendly fight, not killing my opponent would be harder for me, the difficult part here for me would be to just hit him enough to knock out him without taking the life out of him.

 So soon I take a step and so does he as the noise of the crowd go louder, A rabbit in a Lion's den it seems to everyone there. Raaga quickly lifts up his heavy leg and lands it directly on my chest with a thud pushing me at least four steps back pretty near to the end of the ring. His hits have got Power, he hits with Passion, that's one thing for sure as I almost feel a heart attack in my chest, maybe a little harder than that and my heart would have exploded, but it wasn't that hard and my heart is still there beating with life and so am I. So no more taking hits from this Mighty guy anymore after this, it would be quite risky I decide as the crowd chanting Raaga's name goes louder and louder as if by now even a few devils of hell have descended into the sky to chant his name along and to make me feel puny, as they too wouldn't be happy with me as I had sent so many men until today to them in Hell.

I then at once run towards Raaga as he swings his big left arm to bang my head and I quickly duck down to save myself while moving towards his left side giving him a tight fist blow denting my knuckles to his left rib hard enough to fracture it at least. Then still being on his left side I jump and while being in mid air I take the advantage of him being lowered and in pain due to the brutal blow to the rib as I punch him on the face with my right hand that almost blacks him out. This time he takes four steps back.

The crowd is now all quite and shunned, I think I am done for the moment, this much should be enough to not kill a person. So I turn around with my back facing him now and start to walk away. I am just about to leave the ring peacefully when he again calls me

'Aaye...where you going Madarchod?'

He then looks more furious and starts to run towards me like a Mad Bull as I just remain calm, I am like a Monk who can Kill. I turn my body a little and as he comes near with full force, so does my left leg that pushes him far away with a loud smack as I dig the heel of my feet in his puffed up chest. But then too he doesn't give up and tries to run towards me again, as this time I turn my body totally around to face him but while swinging my right leg as he comes near and then lands in contact with the thunderous hit to his face from the unexpected quick swing of my right leg. This kick of mine maybe would have burst up a football. There at once the mighty Raaga falls to the ground with a red stamp of my foot on his cheek. It will be there visible for next four days at least. The mark of my victory over him. The mark of the Conqueror.

I do no arrogant show off while standing as the clear winner in the ring over my knocked out opponent. I just again turn away to leave the ring as the none from the crowd says a word, but soon someone calls me again from behind, this time I turn around and there are two men almost same as my height and build, standing in the ring. They are the twins, these are the personal ball lickers of Raaga, somewhat like his bodyguards. So they don't easily swallow seeing their Boss getting defeated in such a terrible way, embarrassing as hell it is for them. So they too make the foolish mistake of thinking that they would kick my ass even after seeing how good I am when it comes to fight as I just did to their Boss, Raaga.

They both run towards me while shouting at the top of their lungs with anger and soon the first twin swings his right hand as I quickly duck down making him totally miss as he goes behind me qwith force. Then I instantly lift my right leg and land my heel hard on the abdomen of the second twin approaching in front of me as he falls far away on the ground on his back.

The twin behind my back then again tries to punch me, but before his hand even reaches me, my right leg of course taller than his hand reaches towards him at my backside as I kick him on the chest without even turning back around. He directly falls into the nearby crowd of prisoners at the border of the ring.

 The twin in front of me until then gets back up on his feet and again while shouting with fury he runs towards me. He then raises his right leg to swing it quickly through the side and maybe puncher my rib which I intentionally take on my body knowing that his hit won't even be as strong as his shouting, after getting hit on the rib I realize that was actually right about his kick not being that powerful as the only reason why I let him hit me is so that I can catch and hold his leg with my left hand near pressed against my rib as he now finds it harder to balance himself on just one leg on the ground. I have a plan for a wonderfully brutal combination at the moment among which the first is to kick him directly at the groin maybe destroying his balls as only then I let go free his left leg near my rib from my hand. He painfully lands on his knee with a face resembling to someone blowing a balloon, but a very big ass hot air balloon. He goes red and before the twin on my back would come to fight back, I punch the twin in front of me who is on his knee directly on to his nose, another thundering punch to his jaw and one more finally on his right eye, knocking him out for good. The twin on my back who I had kicked till the edge of the ring until now comes back and climbs up on my back with his arms around my neck as he keeps clinging to me. The problem for me here isn't the fighting moves they are doing against me, but the constant loud annoying shouting they have been doing since the start as the twin on my back too shouts with anger right into my ear as he still keeps clinging on to me from behind, now that's when I feel like I have had it enough of their high pitch childish shouting which would soon maybe make me lose my sanity and even my hearing. So all I do is hold his arms which are around my neck and shoulder and then just do a sudden left shoulder jerk towards my front as he flies forward and lands on the muddy ground rocking and rolling. He tries to get up again, but before he can, I go ahead and kick him like a football at his abdomen making him go rock and roll once again. Then as he lies down on the ground, I go ahead before he gets up again, keep my left leg on his chest with the intention of exerting all my weight I possibly can on his body as he groans. Then I lift my right leg up from the ground which makes all my body weight fall on the left leg of mine which at the moment is on the chest of him as he groans harder but the noise of it struggles to come due to the obvious congestion in his chest as I stand on it. I instantly kick the toe of my right leg on his left cheek as fresh red blood splatters from his mouth and he too gets knocked out and gone for good like his other twin and the Boss Raaga.

I get off him, turn my back towards my fallen opponents and start to walk away from the ring again. This time no one calls me from behind. This time no one stops me. I pass through the shunned and shocked crowd of prisoners and the guards as they move away making way for the Champion to walk out. Everybody in that very moment fears me so much as if they have seen the death hearself with their own eyes. I am the Death. I am the new Lion. The New Undisputed King of this Jungle. Did anybody just pee in their pants?

LAYLA

I just slept at five in the morning and I am awake like an Owl at Eight. Just three hours of sleep, makes me remember my time when I used to shoot the big budget movies, being a popular actress in demand gives only a pretty few hours to sleep and it doesn't bother you because at the end of the day you are just following your passion and living the dream. Of course along with a fat paycheck. But now waking this early like before feels miserable since I don't have anything to do at hand. I haven't been drinking and physically I feel a lot better. But I can just feel the tale taste of tobacco on my tongue and I cough purposefully to let my fucked up congested smoking lungs breathe. Then I get up and for the first time in a while I feel like doing some hardcore exercise, but my mind is still messy, so I decide to just do some Meditation and Yoga, that is of course after a cigarette and my black coffee. I take a shower and put on my yoga pants after an eternity. I then do my poses on the yoga mat and sit down meditating and talking to myself about myself after a long time. That's when I realize that why in the world I have been feeling like shit even now.

The thing is that the stranger in the prison has

recently been making a place in my heart and I like that. I do enjoy the thrill and risk involved in making out and giving myself adventurously to a complete stranger who is in a prison serving time and might be a criminal of any kind. But that doesn't seem to trouble me, the thing about love and youth is that they make you go blind and ignorant to the obvious, resulting in heartbreaks and then we blame God. It's quite simple a formula of Nature - where there is Love, there is even Heartbreak.

So it dawns upon me clearly that the unusual bond with that stranger with the ocean eyes has been healing me and doing wonders for my well-being, but if I continue it this way with him and not disapprove his advances, then this can become a rope of trouble in my own neck because no matter how enjoyable and thrilling this might feel to me now, the whatever bond I have with him actually is just Meaningless and utterly Stupid. There of course isn't any future to it and I am young, but not young enough anymore, not the age to fool around with strangers and risk giving them my heart. Now I am old enough to fall in love with someone who can take care of my fragile miserable heart and with whom I can have a future.

I get up, fold my Yoga mat, grab a cigarette and my golden lighter, then go into the balcony again as the rays of the golden sun just emerged a few hours ago hit me as if they have been here as long as time and never ever had gone after dusk. I light up and look at the new life of the town as the day starts and the hustle bustle of the city of dreams - Bombay where everyone either in a car, foot, bus or train seems to be in a hurry to win at life, but unfortunately only a few will. There are no more people far away sleeping on the the side of foot-paths, those guys would now either be doing their begging on the street job or they would be pull-ing heavy handcarts to transport the loads or just any other job they would have. Everybody works hard.

Yesterday night like a teenage girl, I was just thinking about that prisoner stranger with whom I have kissed twice and was maybe falling in love with him in my thoughts, but now as I stand here in the same balcony of mine, I decide that this can no longer go on, whatever this has been, it has to end. I am a mature grown up woman now and should think like one. That would be good for both of us, Not that I care for him too much, but at least I care for myself.

I extinguish my cigarette and get the urge to throw it down from my this 24th balcony and I do as the only remaining butt of the smoked cig-arette wavers in the air here and there and goes away to fall off somewhere far. In the next session I will talk to him and make him understand what's real, I might even scare him with my contacts and reach if needed so, well that's a different thing that none of my contacts and in my reach would presently answer my phone let alone help me, still what does he know. I will make everything right and talk to him, so that he doesn't bother me again. Will get the idea of Love out of his mind. But I will definitely have to be careful to not create any sort of a scene and give the gossip media anymore juicy negative news about me. I will have to act like in the role of a no bullshit very angry strict woman with him. That should scare him....I hope so.

CHARLES

I am kissing those luscious lips of hers again with my hands all around her, I have my eyes closed and there is not a part of her soft body which until now has not been touched and explored by my sinful hands. I grasp her tighter and keep kissing with all the passion inside of me, then I open my eyes and see ourselves standing in a passageway of some building with white walls and too many orange colored sun rays coming in here as if either right now the sun has just risen or is about to go down, Furious dusk or the Coolly Dawn. I still keep kissing the love of my life and then out of nowhere behind her there approaches a man. He just walks in slowly, stands there far away behind her and then whispers her name as miraculously even the dull whisper still reaches here to us from that far. The guy looks like he is wearing a well fitted black tuxedo, but his face is just too blurry and I can't see it no matter how hard I try and force my eyes to. Then he whispers her name again as I try to hold her tighter in my arms so that he would never ever be able to take her away from me.

That's when I feel a strong sudden pain in my stomach and I feel my grasp on her loosening. The pain in my stomach almost feels as if somethings tearing up my intestines and grows so stronger that I eventually end up on my knees. I look down and see blood on my shirt even though there is no cut or any bruise on my abdomen, yet I bleed tremendously as I touch to check any wounds and there isn't any. Now I have even blood of mine on my hands and I feel scared and so afraid for the first time ever. Not afraid of death, but the fear of losing her. Afraid of not being abled enough for the moment to keep her with me and then she without turning back while just looking into my eyes with a mean smirk starts to take steps backwards in the direction of that tuxedo man calling for her from far away at the back.

 The insufferable pain grows further as I soon fall on the ground and my vision gets too blurry almost as if I would have my last breath any second now. I helplessly just look at her then turning while walking up to that unknown man in a tux as she hugs him hard by wrapping her thin arms around his neck and he then greedily grabs her into his arms as if their bodies were made for each other since the beginning of time. Then they go away while holding each other's hands and I feel life going out of me as I too whisper her name 'Layla' with the very little struggling voice left in me for the last time before passing out to another world feeling a last wet drop of tear on my cheek along with the last breath. Dying with her name fresh on my lips, what more could I ask?

Everything is black and dark for me then. Nothing more. By now the tears on my cheeks would have dried up I assume.

That's when I get up. A nightmare it was.

Here I am up wide awake now with so much sweat all over my body as if I had just run too many a miles. The prisoners in my cell are still asleep and the sky outside has a very slight hint of blue as if sunrise would happen soon as I watch through the small opening space at the top of the prison wall.

This was not just a nightmare. Telling it a bad dream would be more than just an understatement. This felt like sadness, pain, heartbreak and death all combined with the sudden blow of coming back to life and reality in just a moment. God knows how my brain handled it all and didn't just explode. There is a reason the mind cannot Comprehend so many things of the Universe. One such thing is Love.

LAYLA

I park my white BMW outside the gate and enter the Byculla prison for my drama class. Today I am a good thirty minutes early before the class starts, so its 9:30 am and I as usual first go into my green room which is next to an empty cell just in front of the open courtyard. They do not even have an air conditioner in here but at least the fans run at good speed at their fullest. I sit down and ask a hawaldaar guard to bring me a cup of tea which he further orders to an adolescent tea seller boy whom they call Chotu. Chotu might be something 15 or 16 as there is not the slightest sign of hair or beard on his thin face. He always like others looks at me in awe and awkwardness as if he hasn't seen a woman ever before or maybe a woman who is a top actress in Bollywood. Chotu brings two small glasses in his small netted basket, one with water and the other with tea, I skip the water one, god knows if it is even filtered or not. I sip my tea and take out my cigarette as Chotu still stands there staring at me mindlessly until I look into his eyes and he immediately leaves or runs away you could say.

As I smoke and sip tea, I once again call in the hawaldaar guard and ask him to bring that stranger prisoner. At first he seems confused to whom I am referring since I don't even know his name but then I make it clearly understandable for him when I say

'That guy who did the good act with me on the stage that day, remember?' I ask

'Oh that one, I will get him right away madam ji' he replies obediently but along with it I sense some quirkiness on his face as if he thinks I am calling in that stranger prisoner so that we could fuck here in my green room. God how horrible would that be and I would obviously never fuck him anyway.

The guard leaves to fetch Him for me and until I am done with my cigarette, there is a knock on the door to which I reply

'Get in'

There he walks in as I without even looking at him say

'Lock the door'

It would be the most stupidest thing ever to deliberately get yourself locked in a room with a criminal, but to my surprise there is not even the slightest fear in me and I just feel so in control at the moment of the situation. I am just following my intuition, and I guess my years as the top lady in the movies has made me all this bossy and egoistic.

He locks the door and then comes to stand right in front of me and I had until now made up the decision in my mind that no matter what happens, not to look in his hallucinating eyes. So I keep looking else where and everywhere other than his eyes and I am pretty sure he is just constantly looking at me now. I ask him to sit down on a plastic chair a little far to the side of me as I take out another cigarette before speaking

'You know whatever we did in the previous sessions, I do not know what it was, but I want to make it clear to you that for me it meant nothing' I say while looking down on my feet to avoid his eyes and I keep taking the puffs of my cigarette so that I remain calm and as practical as possible for the moment

'And I want even you to understand that it was nothing, imbibe this in yourself that it was just fucking mistake on my side and nothing else. Think or consider it as a dream and just forget it. Because if any of us thinks that it was something more than nothing, than we both will be in deep shit trouble. You get me?' I ask while accidentally looking up right into his EYES.

He doesn't reply anything and keeps looking at me with the slightest of a smile on his lips. I was supposed to say something more, but my mind feels as if it has just been turned off like a switch and all I can possibly do for the moment is to keep looking at him in his ocean eyes and feel myself drowning. Fuck! Why did I look up at him? He soon realizes the long pause I have taken and my helplessness as he gets up from the plastic chair, walks up to me, bends down leaning towards me with his hands on the armrest of my chair and his beautiful face so near to mine. He just keeps smiling and looking into my eyes from this "closer than near" distance as now I can even see myself as I have never seen before in the reflection in the pupil of his eyes - The Dreamy Layla Rathod with her eyes wide opened mindlessly staring back at her as if she is drowning in an Ocean of Paradise and she sure is loving every bit of the death from the waters of Love in it.

 I totally lose it like the previous times and before I can realize, I have my eyes closed and my lips kissing every single inch of his face with my both hands behind his head running through his coarse hair. He for sure even now is staring at me like I am A Goddess with his Ocean eyes.

 Only if I had been a Goddess then I would have without any doubt made him the King of The Oceans and all the water there ever is.

That's when he picks me up from my chair and then further holds the back of my hips in his strong arms with my legs around his waist and my arms still around his neck to support myself as we do the kiss of death and then while still holding me up in his arms, he walks and then puts me down hard on my dressing table as he moves away all the scattered makeup stuff of mine on the table with his hands as everything falls down to the ground. He kisses me harder and almost bites my lip before moving his face back to remove his black stripped white prison t-shirt. Then continues to kiss me on my neck like a hungry animal while rubbing his right hand on the inner skin of my thighs as I melt further while tightening my legs around him as he stands making love to me while making me sit up on the dressing table. He touches the wet tip of his tongue on my earlobe and for that very moment I am all his to take.

 Sooner than I can realize, he has even got his pants off and we are already fucking passionately. Fucking raw with so much passion as if we are the first and the last of the humankind to ever do so. I don't know for how long we go on like that because till now all I can feel is his rhythmic to and fro motion inside of me and the heat and sweat on our bodies as our fingers slip from the moist skin of each other when we touch now, So for now we just seem to be lost, lost in each other, it looks like we are just too near to each other touching as hard as we can, but in reality only we know that we are totally inside of each other for the moment. Making Love as if the future of humanity and it's existence depends on it.

Even though his pace is making him go breatheless now and I can feel his warm heavy breath, he holds me tighter and keeps going on faster and I now can't resist moaning loudly with pleasure as I too dig deep my feet in his ass cheeks. There is no way anyone if present in the courtyard outside would not here my screams of passion. He keeps thrusting with all he has got as the Sense of time and reality everything seems meaningless and lost for good, his electrifying fingers slowly touch while rubbing the space between my back and it feels as my vertebrae just felt a shock of love giving chills to my soul deep inside. He does all this small arousing things so perfectly as if he has already practised it a hundred times, knowing exactly when, where and which part of me to touch to get me to moan for him in his ears as I finally give in the urge to bite the tip of his left ear. Even though my body is smaller than him in size, for the moment we keep fucking, it is like I have totally absorbed and imbibed every bit of him inside me. Seeing him go so crazy and wildly lusting like a primitive caveman to make love to me further arouses me. The moment like the other moments before with him feels like an eternity and timeless until...

Until there is a sound at the door and we instantly get forced into our own realities as we quickly move our lips and body a little away while looking at it, there is someone twisting the steel knob trying to get it opened. When we don't respond, then there is a knock. I don't care who ever it is, but thank God we had the door locked. Otherwise, this was going to be real bad for both of us as the knocking continues and I answer

'Give me a minute'

Then the knocking stops as then I look at Him as he puts on his clothes, gives me a cute grin and says

'I Love You'

I don't say anything and keep looking at him as he waits a reply from me, then he comes closer to my face again for a kiss. A small kiss and then I finally reply as he again says 'I Love You'

'But I don't even know your name yet'

He smiles again and winks with a boyish charm. Then walks towards the door and leaves.

CHARLES

I go inside and stand with all the other 50 prisoners in the hallway waiting for her, soon she comes in looking all ready again and then we start with the drama class. The whole session again she tries to not look at me. Why does she do that? I don't get it, she just seems to avoid an eye contact with me intentionally, whereas I look like a stupid clown who just keeps looking at her the whole time as she instructs and teaches us the group. Her gestures and her expressions seem perfect enough as if had been practised a hundred times and are tailored with the sole purpose to get any man watching fall right for her.

So today we have to do the stage group acts. Five acts total, Five groups there are. So all the groups one by one go on to the stage and do some bullshit act, which maybe is a serious one, but all the ones watching can't help but wholeheartedly laugh. Considering all the fifty prisoners of this jail, the five groups were distributed equally with ten men in each in the start when this task of group act was given. But now only two groups are full with ten men. Rest of the groups are all now short of men.

First group is one man short and has only nine

men doing the act since its my group and they didn't make me a part of it or involved me in any way and I too wasn't even a bit interested in doing it. They didn't give a fuck, so Didn't I. Fair enough. And of course none among the guards or anyone else thinking himself superior would have had the courage to force me to. After that wrestling tournament, you could say that I am the unofficial Lion of this Wild Jungle becuase the previous Lion Raaga and his two sidekicks are still taking bed rest and haven't recovered enough from their fractures and wounds to get back up. It was a vicious beating and a brutal destruction I had brought upon them in that wrestling ring. So that's the reason the second group is three men short today and has got just seven fools doing the act.

A third group is missing two men and that's the other two beaten and bedridden vicitims of the wrestling match who got smacked by Raaga before I had stepped in.

When a group acts on the stage, the rest sit down on the chairs to watch them bullshitting as if a circus is going on. She just stands below the stage watching the acts and I have a good time watching her watching them with her round beautiful eyes. She looks like a whole moon herself. There are several Artists in the world, but she looks like a whole Art herself. Her cheeks right now seems more redder with make up, the same cheeks which I had madly kissed a while ago. Damn I had messed up her pretty good in there, she was thirsty for so much more, but looking at her now, none would realize that. Hair and face all perfectly made in those ten minutes she took to come here after me.

Even though she is utterly disappointed in all the acts, she makes sure to clap cheerfully for each group once their respective act ends, to encourage and motivate them, that's her job after all. She's a pro at faking it.

LAYLA

Round dark eyes, I have still got some beauty left in me even after my long time habit of chain smoking and drinking, but I have reduced my nicotine intake considerably and cut the alcohol almost to zero, god I don't even do the other huff-puff stuff like the other biggies like me. Well I did, but just thrice in a year maybe, they were on the other hand addicted. Not everyone though, some would totally avoid, some were trying to escape and just a few pretended or maybe actually had their drug addiction under their total control. My usage was so less that it wasn't ever actually an issue for me. But yeah, nicotine, alcohol and stress aren't any less of an enemy of a person. They would take you to the grave and make sure you look as ugly as a ghost while going down in it, but those bad habits have so considerably reduced for me now.

Guess that's why as I see myself in the mirror of dressing table in my bedroom, I can see my cheeks have become better, my eyes look more awake and sharp, complexion much moist and much clearer and glowing than it normally is even though presently I don't have a pinch of artificial makeup on my face. I used to be really pretty back in my teens, I remember that, good looking enough to get any lad die over me. But then work, stress and heartbreaks fucking destroyed me from inside.

Now, I feel better. Not only because of the reduced smoking and no alcohol, but because that Stranger in the Prison makes me feel loved, makes myself feel good about myself, I am in love with myself after a long time. But I know we need to be matured and all that passionate intimacy stuff with him could be Dangerous for both of us. But I tried this time and I know how it ended, so I guess we both can't help ourselves from not getting too touchy and keeping our hands off each other. At least if this has to go on, whatever this is, I need to know his name, about his identity, from where is he, what does he do professionally and what crime in the world he had committed that got him here? Just because he looks like a Snack doesn't mean I should blindly gobble him up. I really need to ask all those questions to him for sure next time when I see him. What if he is just a serial killer or a psychopath rapist who just seduces beautiful women, manipulates them for his sexual desires and then kills them coldblooded once his goals have been accomplished? God, I seriously need to know about him.

I am just thinking about my stranger lover while looking at my prettier glowing self and somewhat rosy cheeks in the mirror and that's when my

Iphone buzzes. I look at it and it's from an unknown number. I do think twice but then realizing I have nothing to lose anyway these days I just pick it up considering someone willing to give me work or new opportunities would be calling me, but as soon as I pickup, there on the other end a voice comes and I more than quickly remember it, it is the voice of my destruction. He says a hello and I go silent. Why in the world has he called me now?

"Hello, are you there?" speaks Johnny Singh again

I still don't say anything, I almost feel like crying and pulling my hair

"Hey, I know you are there, I just called up to ask how you doing these days you know?"

And then he goes dead quite and all I can hear is his breath, his heavy disgusting breath. What the fuck does he mean by that? Why in the fucking world did he had to call now? After all this time? If he would have actually cared then he would have called long back, moreover he wouldn't have left me at the first place. There is so much anger, so much frustration in me at the moment as tears almost come out of my eyes as now I try to speak but there isn't any voice in me anymore. I try harder and feel my voice cracking, so then I take a deep breathe and calmly reply with all the little voice I can manage realizing his heavy breath still there waiting on the other side of the line

"Hello, I am fine. I am good" I say as I feel a fire in myself bursting and volcanic tears wet on my cheeks which looked pretty just a moment ago.

"Well, I was thinking that we should meet up. I wanted to see you for a long time" he says as soothingly as he can with an apologetic tone because obviously his male ego won't allow him to apologise directly.

"Huh?" I ask totally baffled, still giving him another chance to say the obvious apology

"Umm...just come to my place and see me whenever you can. We will sort everything out, I promise" he assures me the same way he used to do before, long time before I had become addicted to him.

"Okay" I say plainly without letting any of my emotions being noticeable in my tone

"Okay? Umm...you take care then" he says realizing the fact that how angry I am at him. He already would have expected that before calling me.

I am getting a strong irresistable urge to say a bold "Fuck You" to him but instead my mouth just whispers "Take care" and I quickly cut the call. God at least I shouldn't have said "Take care" at the end. He would have got the idea for sure, from me trying to be mean to him now.

Oh come on this Son of a bitch Arsehole has a

got a lot of nerves to even call me after all he has made me go through. On top of that he now even asks me to come and see him at his home. Well fuck you Johnny Singh, I am definitely coming to your home that's for sure, and even if I come then it would be because after your this call I just wouldn't be able to control my anger and would come inside your house and stab you with a big kitchen knife at least a 28 times. Or maybe 29.

I look back into the mirror of my dressing table and all I can now see is the black mascara of mine ruined due to the tears as the black water too has reached till my cheeks. I still try not to cry and then I shout at myself in the mirror, that's when I et it all go. I shout and cry as loudly and as much as I want to. I take the yellow flower vase next to my bed and throw it on my tile floor, I then take the lamps and break them too. Then I take a cigarette and go off into my balcony to have a silent peaceful smoke with still the ruined black mascara on my cheeks and around my eyes making me look like an evil witch maybe. But who cares? I'm not the Evil one here.

CHARLES

Birds are chirping, I have now started to like and quite enjoy their this everyday early morning melodious sound. I am sure the birds right now would be on the branches of the long trees a little away from the boundary walls of this prison, the same boundary walls which I failed to climb weeks back. A few dim rays of the new sun are coming in though the little window like open space on the top of our prison wall. I am awake, this is still our sleeping time, at least half an hour more before the guards wake us all up. But I did sleep, not that I have been awake like this the whole night, I slept for maybe the two third of the night and then the excitement of today being another drama session and getting to see her again has kept me thinking and awake since then. A part of my heart she is which goes for two or three days away from me everytime.

So after I have just had my breakfast meal, a hawaldaar guard comes again like the previous time and asks me to come with him.

'Chal, Mem Saab bula rahi hai tereko'

He takes me to that room of her's right in front of our huge courtyard. The Jail Courtyard is just right there as you enter the gate of the prison which is a long metallic door, this courtyard of ours always during the day time has got a lot of sunlight falling on it since it is quite in the open and has no shelter above it. But to reach to this courtyard we the people of this prison which is the guards and us prisoners have to walk through the dark passageway which doesn't have a hint of light, it is dark as the most bottom pit of the hell. So when ever anyone crosses this passageway and just has a step out of it towards the courtyard, sudden burst of so much sunlight almost hurts the eye, getting your palms up to cover up your eyes once out of the passageway has become a subconscious reflex action for all of us staying here. It's the eyes that always take time to adjust to the New Light.

 So after a knock, the guard twists the handle of the door to open it for me and I go in as he leaves. Inside she is waiting for me while smoking a cigarette with her red full lips and long ironed hair kept open today as she looks at me like a Goddess through her round dark eyes with blue colored eyelids with the smoke coming out of her delicate mouth. There are some people on this green earth who have got such big thick lips which look wierdly ugly to many and drop dead gorgeous to just a few crazy ones. But the thing is that the few crazy ones get so badly attracted to those heavy heavenly juicy lips, that if by luck they get a taste of those they wouldn't ever compromise with someone with thinner lips. That's the thing with women who got those big fat lips, if you look at them properly, it will take a while and quite an effort to stop staring at those thirstily. I'm the crazy one who after looking at them, find it harder to look at other places of her body which too are an epitome of beauty. She is seating comfortably on her big chair and is already facing me as I walk in, she is wearing blue colored kurti shirt whose length is till her knees and black leggings. In the centre of her blue kurti from the top of it till the bottom, there is a lot colorful shiny embroidery. The fitting of her clothes make the shape of her body look more beautiful than it even actually might be without them. I sit in front of her and she gives me a faint smile, today she looks confident, she has been making a good eye contact today for the first time, as if today is the only time that she is in her total consciousness and control while looking into my eyes.

'Who are you?' she asks

'Huh?' I reply confusingly while turning around my plastic chair and sitting on it in an unconventional way with my chest leaning on the backrest of the chair as my arms lay on the top of it.

'I mean What's your name? Tell me about yourself, I need to know about you. Lets start with your name?' she inquires while adjusting herself on her big chair without ever letting that slight notorious kind of smile on her face fade away even for an instance.

'Well I will tell you my name, that is only if you want to know, as I don't have any problem with myself telling it to you. But the thing is that until now I am quite certain that you would have imagined me and given me a name in your head in your thoughts, that's one thing I am pretty sure about, so I don't know what that name is but until now you considering me that someone in your mind with a name you yourself would have given me, everything has been going great for me with that particular name. So I would rather suggest that you call me with it and if you aren't comfortable with calling me that out loud, then like until now you can just keep imagining and relating me to that name and identity in your mind. I would love for both of us to be in this Fantasy of ours.' I reply while now getting up from the plastic chair and start to take small gradual steps towards her

Her eyes follow my eyes everywhere and in every moment I make as she again smiles wide as she fully understands what it is I am about to do next, then I again ask her

'So what do you call me in your mind huh? The prisoner Lover? Aashiq Kaidi? The Prisoner Who Loves Me? Unknown Jail Lover? Did I guess any of them right ??'

I ask as she breaks into a laughter with her hands

over her face, then she moves her head sideways indicating a no.

'Just tell me your real name!' she commands again

Until now I have reached quite near to her and am almost standing on top of her as she looks directly up to me sitting on her chair. I then bent down and kiss her cheek firmly as she continues looking at me even in such closeness. Then I bring my face right in front of her and whisper

'Charles, my names Charles. And I love you Layla' I say while looking into each of her eye one at a time since focusing on both eyes together from such closeness ain't possible, from such extreme closeness drowning only in one of her eye at a time is possible. So I whisper again

'I love you, it doesn't matter who I am or what I do, all that matters is that I love you and you love me too, that's enough and more than either of us needs to know.' I say with a smile and her face is all red blushing with no hint of any smile now. Then I go ahead and suck those luscious lips of her with mine. I was dying for them. They are irresistible and magical. I am not going to leave any chance at hand to cherish the nectar of those.

I take up my hands and hold her pretty face, the face with a chiseled jawline and high cheekbones, the face structured properly enough to get any boy crazy over her. As if the God himself made her with such precision to fulfill sole purpose of making it difficult for the men and their hearts to not have her. So holding her face, her cheeks gently in my palms as we kiss, I feel the luckiest and the happiest man alive. This is More than just Life. This is what Paradise tastes like.

I feel her hand touch my neck as her fingers smoothly slid through then grasping the back of it. Her other hand is then felt rubbing on my chest as she slowly slides it till my stomach as I am still standing in front of her and leaning down as she sits and instantly to my surprise I can feel her hand over my trousers grasping my balls tight, my right hand by now has come from the left cheek of her face down to her left breast as I squeeze it and we both moan in love with our eyes closed.

The sound of a twist of the door knob and the door opens, we both quickly move away from each other as if hit by an electric shock. So this time unfortunately we forgot to lock the door and the intruder who has just opened the door didn't even have the decency to at least knock before coming in, but right now we can't even blame hm directly for not knocking the door because first thing is that the intruder more than most probably has seen us making out and the second thing is that the indecent intruder is none other than the mighty Raaga as now he stands near the opened door looking at us confused with eyebrows furrowed and mouth with an open pout.

Why the fuck was Raaga coming in in Layla's dressing room at the first place though?

What in the world work would he have with her that he walked in here right now? Or was he just in here to call her for the drama session? Then why didn't the hawaldaar guard come here to call instead of him? I'm pretty confused my self and then Raaga starts to walk towards us as now Layla gets down from the dresser table and stands right behind me. Raaga keeps walking and shouts furiously

'You little bitch, you fuck him, but you won't fuck me?'

Like a tall monster with a baby of an evil devil inside him, he rushes towards Layla with the baddest of the intentions visible in his eyes and before I can stop him, he pushes me aside with his huge palm on my face, then his hand is raised and just in mid air about to touch her. But I don't let his evil hands fall on her, never ever would I let something happen to her, I quickly kick my left foot on his left knee and as it makes him fall down on that knee, I quickly with my fist of steel, punch him in his face indenting his cheekbone to destroy it once and for all. I then try to go for another punch to knock him out, but he quickly catches my punch in his huge hand and gets up back on his feet as he then starts to push me with his other big palm on the centre of my chest. Unfortunately my first punch didn't do as much damage as I expected it to do. With his forceful push quickly and too harshly my back smashes the wall behind my plastic chair as the intensity and force of his heavy weight body along with is not at all manageable for me.

 Even after me hitting the wall he still keeps pushing me into it as if I would pierce through it, but then his hand on my chest quickly grasps my neck and that's when I feel myself breaking. A few more seconds of his hardcore brutal grasp on my neck and I would be breaking my contact with this world. The choke from an ancient Giant it feels like as eventually his grip on my neck gets so firmly planted that my legs are no more on the ground and he has picked me up in the air pinned to the wall. While holding me tight and static with force, he tries to throw a punch with his other free hand on my face to smash my skull into the wall. But I pick my left hand and put my elbow in front of my face instantly to protect my self as his heavy punch lands on my left bicep. His direct attacks from such close proximity are quite hard with enough ferocious force that if I block two more of his direct hits with my bicep, then even my that whole arm would tear, break or fracture for sure.

 I feel my eyes popping out and the life out of me being pulled as my body struggles for air, so reflexively I strike my right hand on his arm holding my neck, but since that doesn't affect much, I then with the forearms of my both hands strike with all I have got at his huge arm together at once with force and now my neck is finally free from his suffocating strong grasp as I drop back on my feet gasping for the holy breathe of life.

With eyes big enough to show me how angry he is, he again comes at me swinging his arm to punch as I quickly duck down to save myself and his heavy hand hits and almost cracks the wall right behind me. Meanwhile, I take the opportunity and land a sudden harsh blow to his right rib with the pure intention of fracturing it with my knuckles as it is pretty evident that I did hit him hard and at the right spot when I look up at his painful miserable face. Who would believe that just seconds ago I was about leave the face of this planet?

Layla still stands behind us near her dressing table looking at us in shock, she just doesn't realize what to do for the moment. Maybe she just isn't used to this kind of real brutal fights and now her mind can't figure out what is to be done, so she chooses just to stand and watch us bewildered.

I spare no second as Raaga takes a step back in pain while keeping his palm over his almost cracked rib, I quickly jump on my plastic chair near to me and taking from there another juml as a sudden propulsion to strike from up high and land on Raaga's ugly nose, a knock out face destroying punch.

So my skull crusher punch from the air shakes him to the soul as he trembles on his feet and is almost loosing balance now as I land on my feet ready as fuck for attacking him again, everything going dizzy and blurry for him in the head now as he takes uncontrolled steps backward while keeping his palm over his skull where I just smashed my seasoned knuckles. Of course his nose starts to bleed then, most probably I have even broken it.

I wink at Layla to make her feel calmer in this situation as she gives just a struggling slightest smile and then I hurriedly go behind the giant Raaga to strike the heel of my foot, right at the back of his knee which again makes him land down on his that knee. Now it's my turn to grasp and hold his neck as I put my strong arms around his thick neck from behind to strangle him at least unconscious. But this guy doesn't give up yet, his only motivation right now is to knock me off and then lay his hands on Layla, lust of that kind makes a person dangerous enough like a monster, last time when I fought him in the ring, he was just an unmotivated crazy animal, but now he is not same anymore. Now he wants to fuck. The extent to which an animal would go to shamelessly to fulfill it's most primal need.

So the tall Raaga gets up on his feet instantly with me hanging on his back with still my arms around his neck and then he starts to run backwards towards the dressing table. Layla is smart and quick enough to reflexively move in the inch of a second as Raaga with me like a chimpanzee on his back, smashes me onto the mirror of the dressing table cracking it. He again moves a little forward with me and again smashes me on to the large oval mirror, this time totally breaking it among with all the make up accessories at the table which either get destroyed or fallen off on the ground. Now I let go of his neck and feel immense pain in my back. Entrapped in an extreme agony of savage misery I am and is my spinal cord broken or what? I don't know at the moment, there's so much going on now to comprehend that but my back is hurting way too much. Layla standing a little away to my right watches in horror with her hands over her mouth, the dramatic awe-struckness.

 The monster Raaga now turns around to face me and I while still sitting on the dressing table with small pieces of glass either inside the flesh of my back or would have cut me most probably, plant my heel on his chest and kick him. That makes him go back two steps away as I quickly pick up the metallic chair of Layla on which she normally sits and smashes it onto Raaga when he comes again towards me. I had picked the chair up from the arm rest of it and hit first with the back of the chair, but that does hit him, but not hard enough. So this time I try to hit him with the crispy sharp edged bottom of the chair, but mighty Raaga doesn't let it touch or damage his body as he quickly holds the chair in the grasp of his large palms and pulls it away with force from my hands while looking at me with the reddest face of immense rage as he throws away the chair behind. He then catches the t-shirt of mine from my shoulders and drags me forcefully off the dressing table as I land quick on my feet on the ground. He continues to push me furiously as pretty soon my back again smashes something. This time he pushed me through the wooden door of this green house and it opens towards the outside as we collide and fall off suddenly after hitting the door and forcing it to open.

 I am now fallen on the ground just outside the opened door of the greenroom and he is almost sitting on top of my chest preparing to punch my pretty face to death with his huge fists of iron. But before he can even land his punch, I quickly bring up my two fingers, the middle and the index one of my right hand and hit hard with them two fingers directly on Raaga's Adam's apple. I do manage to attack at the right exact spot and with the right amount of pace and force, but this time too I don't hit hard enough, because right now I not trying to kill him, I am in prison already, so killing would be much easier task for me than fighting and trying to make a person just knocked out, I still control my temptation of coldbloodedly killing him and that's why I just hit him with my two fingers on the Adam's apple of his throat with enough calculated force to at least get him off my chest and fall off a little away from me while choking and going unconscious for at least a few following minutes. And that's exactly what happens next. He chokes with bewildered wide open eyes as if painfully sucking the meat of the Devil of death and almost feels as if his balls have gotten up to his throat as he suffocatingly moves away and falls unconscious in the courtyard.

Layla nervously comes towards the door to have a look at me and then I quickly realise there are a few people unfortunately present on my right. I turn my head to look at them while getting up and see that there around 12-13 prisoners standing there. They all are the cock sucking fan boys of Raaga or his gang members you could say. They just saw me fighting and knocking off their Gang Leader Raaga just a moment ago, so what is going to happen next is very much predictable and obvious for all of us present here. Not even a single hawaldaar guard in sight at the courtyard of ours.

So these 12-13 prisoner men start to run towards me to tear me apart and eat me alive, but I don't feel scared, in fact I am so used to this kind of wild feeling and it has been a while since I got this adrenaline rush, so that I too start to run towards them shouting with excitement and hunger to fight with so many men together after such a Long time. I start hitting them as much as I want, it's all just bone on bone, denting skulls, breaking teeth, cracking ribs with all my combination of punches and kicks as I unleash my own hell upon them, but since they all keep attacking at me altogether at once, pretty soon, I am again on my back at the centre of the muddy courtyard.

 I am fallen on the ground with two guys holding tight my right hand, two guys holding my left, two holding my right leg and two my left leg, there is a guy right above my head pushing down my shoulders and a last guy standing on top of me who is bending down and preparing to punch me to death. So a total of around ten guys holding me locked down not letting me even move an inch, ready to slaughter me. I try to move my hands, my legs, my body, my head, but there is no way I can move even a bit, they all have caught me down tight with all their might. Two people putting all the force of their body on each limb of mine. So the man standing above me punches me hard and almost breaks my nose. The power of the punch is felt harder than expected since I am not even allowed the comfort of moving my head after the impact as the guy keeping his palms on my shoulder blades presses me harder to restrict my movement. More than those punches itself it is the back of my head that aches due to the hard ground beneath it with little stones on it. If I keep taking more punches like these then soon my skull would crack open from behind due to the sudden impacts is what I predict, as I am pinned so hard to the ground, I can now even feel the tiny pieces of glasses inside my back going and cutting deeper in my flesh due to the weight of the person standing right above me.

 He keeps punching me and I keep struggling and vibrating with shivers of pain all over my body like a goat being slaughtered as the men keep holding me tight from all the sides. Soon the man above me punching sits on my chest and then gives me another punch, this time almost dislocating and fracturing my jaw as this punch is the hardest one yet and makes my head forcefully turn left towards the direction of Layla my love who still is standing and watching in shock and horror, knowing very well that even if she wants, there is nothing she can do at the moment. She is almost now about to call for the guards which maybe she should have tried a little earlier than now, but its okay. Surprising unexpected situations like these can make a person completely go still and blank in the mind for a few moments. She looks so worried, tensed for me and starts to cry like a child. Seeing her so concerned and sympathetic for me gives me a surreal feeling as if I just had a sip of the sacred liquid from the secret well of immortality. Because suddenly all my pain and wounds seem to have lost their vulnerable sense of feeling, I am numb from pain and dumb from love. She feels for me, what more could I ask from life and from the God? The punches keep on coming with their intensity and power increasing with each successive one, but I don't care, even if the guy brings a hammer and crushes my skull with the pointest backside of the tool, I just wouldn't flinch and shed a tear when my soul would leave this green earth. I would die the happiest death because on this very green earth will be a female who I have loved with all my heart and she too did the same. Ain't I lucky? Because only a few even get the love back from the person they want from. A Happy Lover and a Lucky Bastard I am.

 So with tears in her ocean eyes she almost shouts for a guard with the intention to help me, but by then I see some moment in Raaga lying on the ground. He soon gets out of his unconsciousness and sits up to look at Layla who terrified at once runs inside her green room and locks the door. She is a smart woman to do that I should say, there is no guard yet in sight even after her shouting.

 Raaga gets up on his feet and starts to run towards the locked door. He tries to twist the door knob for opening it which he obviously fails in even when he tries with much force. Then he takes two steps back and runs towards the door in an attempt to destroy it like a bull. The door does seem strong but Raaga seems Stronger, so it won't be long that maybe after three or four attempts of hitting the door with such thrust it would break into pieces. So now I realise that I need to save her. To do that I will have to unleash my full potential, no more hesitation in killing these men now. The only reason why I am on the floor at this moment all held tight by this so many foolish men and getting beaten up, butchered here so brutally is because I am trying hard to not kill people inside this prison. Being a prisoner in a prison for a crime and killing the prisoners in it, when you have a plan to escape prison later, so not at all a good idea to kill. But to save her, that's the only option I have left.

 So I am totally aware by now that moving my body and using my energy to even try to move with ten guys holding me down tight pinned to the ground would be useless, so instead I first pinch one of the guy's forearm holding my right hand and pinch him as hard as I can with the intention of ripping his flesh off, soon I almost pierce my nails with the pinching into the skin of his forearm as he quickly withdraws back his hand, quickly I drag away my right hand from the grip of the another person holding my hand and then I poke my two fingers into the eyes of the first guy whom I pinched and then I even do the same bloody eye destroying finger poke for the second guy. A mere four seconds was all it took me to get the two men on my right holding my hand "bloody blind" and dragging themselves on the ground horrified in agony and new found darkness as they shout terrified.

 The guy sitting on my chest who has been punishing me with punches constantly until now, again prepares and raises his fist up in the air to pulp down my beat up bloody face, but before his hand reaches my skull, I pull him with my newly free right hand through his shirt collar down towards my face and bite his left ear like a hungry mad animal just unleashed from captivity as he screams with his tonsils of the throat vibrating like an out of tune messed up musical instrument. I feel blood from his ear falling on my face and inside my mouth as I now feel the taste of his fresh bitter blood and shaking body on mine.

 The other men holding me tight on my left arm, legs and shoulder now seem petrified as if just seen a ghost of hell with a chainsaw, but the only thing they have got to do possibly is to hold me tighter.

 The guy on top of me going through excruciating pain is soon thrown to my side by right arm as he shakes heavily and shouts while trying to stop the blood pouring out of his ear. I don't even realise where exactly have I even bite him on the ear, but the pain and blood depicts that it might have been a very delicate soft spot.

 Soon the guy above my head holding me down with his palms on my shoulder blades now try to throw a punch on me, which I quickly dodge my tilting my head a little to the side as his fist misses and hits on the ground, then I with my only free right hand grapple him from behind his head and pull his face down near to mine, then I smash my forehead directly at the centre of his face thrice until I can hear the satisfying sound of the tiny delicate bones of his face breaking as I am assured that at least his nose and front teeth would be gone for good. He quickly moves away and falls on his back on the ground making himself join the shouting with the guys in immense pain group. But there are more participants of the group to join in the cry of agony yet as I give a karate chop to the Adam's apple of the first guy holding my left hand, making him choke to almost death and then I grab the second person holding my left hand from his bushy hair and drag him from left to the right side of my body while smashing his face unto the hard pebble ground, I do that too thrice until again I get to hear the satisfying bone breaking sound. Soothing to my ears, that is music to the eardrums of a Cold Hearted Killer. I am a bloody fucking Musician and bones are my instrument.

The ones remaining and holding my legs almost piss in their pants by now as I get up and sit, I punch one guy and kick another both on their faces, while one more person I just grapple him around the neck with my leg and strangle him with all the force of my strong hamstrings until there is no more movement in his shaking body, so either he is just unconscious or maybe dead, but I don't care whatever it is right now as I need to catch up on Raaga. The remaining 2-3 men just run away to save their lives as Raaga by now has constantly been pushing at the door forcefully with his body and now one more strong push of his crumbles down the wooden door as I had predicted.

Layla is at the far end corner of the room and she shouts with terror with now her eyes closed and hands around her cheek upon seeing Raaga break the door. Damsel in Distress, My Damsel. She can protect herself and mostly she would even know how to fight, these actresses do some fancy martial arts training for their roles in action movies, but here seeing the bull like size and strength of Raaga anyone would be afraid for their life. But of course I am an exception, so as she then opens her eyes and grabs a pointed piece of glass from the shattered mirror on the ground to at least try to defend herself from the evil monster Raaga, who is just about to take his first step inside her green room. By then I have ran and reached in time right behind him as the panic on Layla's worried face now upon seeing me just disappears into thin air with tears on her cheek which would soon dry up. I quickly from behind get hold of his right leg and pull his ankle with immense force, such great instant force that my pull makes him fall harshly direct on his face, smashing his nose on the hard concrete of the outside of the green room's floor. Then with all my might I pull the leg of the fallen Raaga dragging him and almost while struggling swing and throw his damn big body right in the centre of the courtyard. This is the heaviest I have ever lifted. And I don't even think I ever would have been able to lift and throw away someone so heavy, but I am a person in the spell of love doing all this to protect his enchantress. This is the Power of Love.

He groans on the ground and that's when I before leaving his right leg from the grasp of my hand decide to break it forever by kicking him mercilessly at his knee joint.

Then I jump in the air and land a punch right onto his big hairy chest, the most painful final blow of mine as blood spurts out of his mouth dropping on my face. But still the bastard doesn't die as only now the hawaldaar guards come into the courtyard and take hold of me, the only remaining one. Last standing Champion. Where in the fucking world were these guards all this time when we needed them the most? Only now when I have just done the necessary to protect her and overpowered my severely outnumbered enemies, that's when they come? They hit me with the baton sticks as usual and drag me away like an animal, and I let them do that to me as I even see the guards taking Layla out from her green room to safety, her mascara and makeup totally ruined and even in such a worried shaken state, she looks like the most beautiful woman in the world, my Angel Layla as we finally exchange a quick glance and I am dragged away. She is worth fighting for.

LAYLA

I am escorted till the outside of the prison to my White BMW by a policeman and he instructs me to just leave for now as I shiver

"Aap abhi jaao Madam"

I get in my car, switch on the air conditioner and look at myself in the top rear view mirror, I look so shook and scared to death that the makeup on my face is ruined as if I have just done a movie scene in which I see a deadly ghost. I had come here all dolled up and now I look a terrible mess.

I look in front through the metallic gate between the rods of it, I see the injured and almost killed prisoners struggling and crawling on the floor while a few literally groaning and crying in misery. Soaked in their own blood as the guards take them away on stretchers, an Ambulance for sure by now might have been called and would reach soon, but a very few among them will at least die from their injuries, that's for sure. I think to myself 'Oh God, What in the world have I made this man do. All this violence and brutality just because of me, just because I was carelessly, irresponsibly and totally immaturely kissing and making out with a fellow criminal in my green room of a prison, stupidest thing anyone could ever do. I feel so much uneasiness in my chest due to the venomous guilt buiding up in me, morever I did all this even without locking the door. What was I thinking? Or was I even thinking at all?'

 Back in the days when Johnny and I would fight and quarrel over any petty matters, he would often angrily taunt me as a "Dumb Bitch" and that would always piss me off more than ever. But only today for the first time I am considering the thought that maybe he was right?...Aah fuck Johnny...What does that Bloody Bastard know?

 With my mind and engine running, I switch the gears and press the pedal to leave quickly as I know that if I keep on thinking long enough about this, it really won't be any good for me. I would just sink deep into it's darkness. The thing that has happened has already happened and can't be undone. So just thinking about the already done thing and stressing over it now won't do shit.

 I come in my home and directly fall on my face in my bed with open arms. I lay there for a while until I remember that Johnny had asked me to see him today at a resto, kind of a date it is, but obviously it isn't one. He just wants to see me and talk about something he feels important. Although I am pretty more than just shocked from what took place today at the prison, going out to see Johnny would really help me get my mind distracted away from the prison horrors. A part of me hates him and never would want to see the face of the cruel selfish Johnny Singh, but a bigger part of me which will always be in love with that bastard would definitely make sure I always do what ever he wants me to do for him. I am the Prisoner to his Love.

I get up and go to take a shower.

It takes me a good two hours in front of the mirror and after trying a lot of outfits from my collection of innumerable pieces of clothes. At the end after a careful decision while being picky and lots of trying out of so many outfits, I put on a dark black silk leggings with a light brown sleeveless top which is like a mini gown. I get ready. Like the actual get ready, the Gorgeous Layla Rathod after an eternity. I myself get mesmerized by my appearance in the mirror, seeing myself look like that after such long makes me freeze looking at the beautiful me for a while, men on the street would break their neck staring at me. The goal is to go casual and not so over the top while still looking attractive as hell. I take a shot of vodka to calm my fast anxiously beating heart and feel some heat in me, light up a cigarette, put on my big black sunglasses and leave for my date with the worst Heart-breaker, the evil monster and the forever keeper of my heart, Johnny Singh.

CHARLES

I feel excruciating pain in my jaw, most probably I have lost a tooth and can feel the bottom line of teeth in my left jaw loose, almost broken and hanging. I am bleeding, there is blood on my face, I can smell it, it has dried up, the most of the blood is of other men I almost killed and beat the shit out of in the courtyard, but I can feel with enough assurance and pain that some of it is even mine and I cannot even realize now which part of me is cut, wounded and bleeding. I am pretty hurt, that's for sure. But right I cannot even touch my face or my aching body to check any wounds of mine since my both hands are tied with chains on either side high up on the wall almost pulling me apart. I am not standing straight or at all on my feet, I don't have any strength left in me for the moment, the chains have my hands tied high up and they are the only ones pulling me up straight and supporting my falling body. A dark separate prison they have brought me into and kept for now, I can feel myself suffocating with the dried blood jammed in my nostrils and the taste of it on my tongue. A Killer is basically a murderous Carnivore.

So there is not much air in here and an opening

similar to my jail cell behind me high above on the wall. I can see very few rays of the dull yellow moon falling on the black rusty steel bars in front of me, seems like it is not even a half moon out there today.

 Eventually I hear heavy footsteps approaching towards my cell, I most probably know what's going to happen next. Not that I am afraid but still I think "God Save Me", that is if there is any.

LAYLA

I drive to this nearby resto named Shamiana and park outside as I see his blue Mercedes a little away. So he is already inside waiting for me. This resto is just near to my residence and we have had come here a lot of time before to spend a good quality time together. He knows that I love this place, but I guess he still didn't understand to this date, that I love this place only in his company. Without him, even the Greatest Heavens would seem a bore to me.

So as usual, I go into the all orange lighted air conditioned resto and walk out of it through the back door, trying not to meet eyes with the known staff and manager of the place as I pass through the indoor part into the behind open seating place. There are hardly a few customers inside and none outside in the lawn-like seating place of the resto, all natural lighting here. This outside place of the resto behind, has got large umbrellas on top of the tables to cover the customers from the sun. Just in the centre of this outdoor part, there is a beautiful mini fountain built from blue and white colored marble stones. All the four sides of this large outdoor place has got mostly fake bushes, plastic plants and flowers about which obviously I don't give a damn. Artificial grass mats, fuck earthing, everything about here is a dillusion and a lie, even my lover who I am going to meet. The only reason why I prefer this place is because the food is good and too expensive for any average person to come here, plus it is near to my place and the main reason why I like this outdoor part rather than indoor is because smoking is allowed here. There are wonderful glass cut ashtrays kept on all the tables, what else would I need? Aah Ashtrays, My Saviour.

So I walk into the lawn and there I see him seated on a table while tapping his feet on the ground restlessly, he at once stops that on seeing me and stands up with a wide grin.

There he is, my Destruction. My worst enemy and my Best Lover. The one person I hate the most and Love the most. I want to kill him cold blooded right here right now in his sky blue shirt tucked in his grey well fitted pants with the sleeves of his shirt raised till the elbow. He looks handsomely dangerous, God how much I love him even after all he has done to me. I am a fool, the biggest fool ever to live.

He has got nerves for sure as he without any hesitation hugs me tight while greeting as if nothing as ever happened until now and I realize that most probably he knows that how crazy I am for him. Maybe he thinks that he can just kick me away mercilessly like a dog and I would even then come for him running when he would need me, and I fear that maybe he is thinking right about me after all.

We sit down and even though the sun has already set an hour ago I don't yet remove my big sunglasses because by now my eyes are wet and I don't want to show him my tears. I am not going to give him the smooth chance to come near to console and get his hands all over me. But then he holds my hand on the table and I break down completely. Fuck. Am I so weak and vulnerable?

As I predicted that's exactly what he does, he quickly pulls his chair close to mine around the table and puts his one arm around my shoulder to rub it and with another he softly pushes my head on his shoulder to rest and cry on. Reminds me of my old makeup artist who always used to say, that "Whenever men provide the shoulder to cry on, trust me they don't give a damn about your tears Princess, they definitely just want to fuck your brains out."

CHARLES

Fourth time it is that the heavy built guard behind me strikes with his baton stick and this time I shout furiously with tears as again the son of a bitch hits me on my lower back. I am now almost feeling my soul trying hard to escape from my caged body, a few more hits there on my lower back and I would definitely be crippled for life. The guard intentionally or not I don't know, but has been striking hard at my spinal cord. My delicate supporting bone would break if he continues like this and even now I know I will not be able to get up on my feet at least for a week. The lower back is one of the most sensitive places of the body and these bastards even though it doesn't look like from their stupid faces, are maybe aware of that and that's why are targeting it with so much focus, torturing like the deadly devil from the bottom pit of the hell.

He again strikes but this time with the corner round end of his metallic baton stick, as I again shout with immense pain. More than unbearable it seems now as I cry and scream as if I am begging for my life. The tears falling off from my eyes and the saliva from my mouth as I get beaten up helplessly making the blood on my face wet again as the smell of it fills my nostrils.

I never cry, but today I am weeping like nobody I have ever heard. Crying for mercy, not that I am asking mercy from this guard torturing me, if it was in my hands then I wouldn't care even if they cut me open and leave me to die, but here my body automatically is mourning and screaming like a man on fire because of the extreme brutality of the hits. Luckily the guard doesn't hit me anymore for now on my lower back and gives me just a few more hits on my abdomen and my legs, those too are painful, but at least bearable for a strong cold hearted man like me.

The guard hits me more while taunting for the first time

"Fucking that actress right under our nose, you son of a bitch, Gaandu"

He throws a few more hits and hindi abuses at me, then leaves.

That's when I realize that Raaga has said the cops everything he saw, informing the cops is definitely ratting upon. Definitely along with some spice added from his own mind would have narrated the whole story and gossip to these guards. That's what jealousy and hatred makes you do. No wonder this guard kept striking me at my lower back, so that I could not for a long time use the rhythmic motion of my hips to have sex with anyone. I wouldn't be surprised at all if tomorrow they torture and break my balls.

LAYLA

Mini comes in lashing into my room shouting

"What in the fucking world did you think you were doing in that prison?" she asks with her face all red

"You cannot talk to me like that" I reply without a twitch on my face while calmly making small circles of my cigarette smoke as I sit next to the dressing table in my lavish bedroom. I say this with so much coldness in my voice that it makes her realize her position as my assistant, though over the years she has become more of an elder sister to me and we are both aware of that.

She quickly regains her composure and tries to soften up a bit with the rage she came in

"Okay, but why? Why were you making love with a prisoner??" she asks while lowering her voice but still totally trying to sound pissed at me

"Who told you?" I maintain my calmness

"Oh come on, it's all over the news by now. Everybody knows. We are already in deep shit and now this??" she says with helplessness evident on her pretty face. I totally understand that she is not angry at me, but is just concerned like a loved one for me.

"That's all fake bullshit. Rumors it is" I say and take a good big puff to get that filthy tobacco hit hard in my lungs. Gosh I just wish a vein of mine just gets blocked with the tar and kills me already.

"Layla, the Inspector from the prison called me up, he told me all this. No more drama classes from now on. The only job we had and even that's gone now. He said you were having an affair with someone there, but the bastard told me late, late after all this is Breaking News on the TV, on every damn channel, these media guys love defaming someone. They are crazy for juicy gossip and you always don't fail to give them. Do you even think about your reputation?" she asks and now I start to feel like I am losing it. My heart starts to beat faster and my cigarette is almost over till the butt. So I quickly extinguish it in the glass ashtray and light up another with my shaky hands while re-plying to her without meeting her eyes

"I don't care, it's all fake. Lies they are."

"So you won't even tell me the truth now?" she inquires with a hint of politeness and sympathy while asking again

"No, Mini. This is what we are supposed to say to the Media. The News people, that it is all fake, without sound proof soon the news will be a rumor and rumors don't last long, ineffective they are darling. You know." I say and then finally look at her. I can see her sweating from the forehead as she stands in front of me.

 "Oh, so that you have already figured it out? Trust me babe, you have no idea about these media people, it is not that easy, even if it is the most obvious lie, if there is enough juice and TRP from it, these News guys would leave no stone unturned and give it their all to make it a wonderfully enjoyable and a quite believable circus for the audiences. After all we have been through until now, I am quite surprised that you don't understand it all yet. And are you saying you had the solution in your head since the starting of your Love making affair in the prison with that guy?" she asks while rolling her eyes annoyed and I take a deep breath before she again continues

 "Okay, but why Layla? Why an unknown prisoner? I get it, the flings, they give a thrill, but Fling with a criminal in a jail, why?" she asks and seems to be almost crying

 "You wouldn't get it" I reply and get up from my seat to walk towards her

 "I wouldn't get it? What do you mean?" she almost shouts and I firmly grab her by the arm to take her towards my bed as we sit next to each other close. I then put my head on her shoulder and speak

"The matters of the heart Mini. Nobody can explain and nobody can understand"

The dialogue I say to her sounds really good cinematically and quite deep, would definitely win awards and claps if in a movie, but sitting here in real life, we both know that this time we are really fucked.

CHARLES

Two whole most gruesome days of merciless and constant torture as if punishing me for the crimes of all of the mankind together. Late at night, they would take off the tight chains of my bruised wrists and I would instantly fall on the ground like a large sack of wheat. Then a guard would bring me just a few slices of hard bread and some water in the name of food. Just one meal a day now and that too in such small quantity, fucking my appetite, food isn't being given to me to fill my stomach but to just keep me alive for more torture. So that they can enjoy hurting me without any consequences because I would be so weak that I wouldn't be able to attack back in case I get a chance and the idea to.

So today is the third day since I had not seen her and had been tortured here by these ruthless prison guards and officials. After their lots of taunting and abuses on me as they hit with all the strength in their bodies, I now realize why this is being done to me, it took me a while to understand this since most of the things they angrily say and shout at me while hitting just don't go into my ears as I am too preoccupied in my own pain and sobbings of mercy. But now when I think hard, I do have figured it out and the realisation has finally come to my senses of why all this is happening to me. Not because I beat the shit out of so many prisoners, not because I stole the light of the eyes of a few of them by destroying them and made them blind, not because I broke a lot of bones of those fellow prisoners, not because I have caused the injuries worse enough that they had to be taken to hospitals, but the actual reason for the endless suffering being bestowed upon me is totally different.

Behind all this inhuman immeasurable torture and the immense anger in the guards is stinging an ugly truth that I have brutally hurt their male egos bad.

Every man in his own foolish mind considers and sees himself pretty highly. Way more than just pretty highly actually, a person thinks himself to be the best in terms of appearance and cleverness. Everyone feels that they are superior to all the others and are the smartest, cleverest, and the most gorgeous looking thing in the world. That's natural and in the nature of every man, everyone thinks highly of themselves. That's the only way for humans to be sane to survive and have a zest for living life. That natural quality would be the only reason for them essentially taking care of themselves.

So when these egoistic prison officials and guards

got to know from Raaga that the most beautiful actress in the world has been in Love with me, but not with them, it hurt them pretty bad. They obviously see me way inferior to them in all terms, so they are angry individually just because the actress didn't get attracted towards them, instead she fell for an insignificant prisoner who they think is the dust of their feet.

 Even Raaga was infuriated on seeing us making out in the green room that day for the same reasons I am sure, he might have thought that why in the fucking world would this woman become so close to me and not with the well built huge himself.

 They think that even in their highly presence, the woman fell for the lowly me. Swallowing the truth has become harder for them, and to ease the pain of swallowing the ugly truth, they have been beating the shit out of me savagely.

LAYLA

Today I got to know from Mini that Johnny and his wife have secretly completed their divorce a week back. It was his wife who had filed the divorce months ago and now she was finally free, I am sure her lawyer would have gotten her a very good bargain in alimony at Johnny's expense. This all was kept so lowkey and confidential that none except for the very close ones to each of them were the people knowing about it and that's why it took a week for the news to reach till Mini from her friend. It was kept so secretive so that as always the media wouldn't be able to enjoy the news for TRP and hence not be able to give unnecessary bullshit gossips to the audiences who always were hungry for news of someone else's personal life. Average people love watching the downfalls and destruction of famous successful people.

That's when it dawned on me why had Johnny been wanting to see me that day and today too I have got a text from him for an another date. He again wants to talk something important. Last time he had just told me that soon he would get me a role as the lead heroine in one of his upcoming movies, will set things straight for me and told me that he had been feeling quite guilty to make me go through all that he had. I couldn't figure out if he actually meant all those things he was saying but he continued to speak that I didn't deserve any of these troubles and sufferings, so now he would try his best and as much as in his ability and power to get things up and back running good smooth for me. He promised me and although I tried my best to not show it, it did feel good on hearing that. I didn't push any further, A egoistic man and a Moviestar at his peak with the status like him, that's more than enough of an apology coming from him. But what even surprises me more now is the fact that he didn't even give me a hint of the divorce thing going on with his wife, didn't even utter a word about it.

Now from Mini I got to know that they settled it as such that the wife would keep the custody of the daughter and even got something close to 4 million for it while Johnny still would be allowed to visit the daughter once a week at the wife's newly bought duplex apartment. 4 million might look like a big amount, but here it actually is not. Definitely Johnny's lawyer would have been a top cunning fellow who got him such a cheap bargain in this one. Come on, he is the Richest and Among the biggest movie star in our industry, his net worth might be at least around 300 million, I estimate from what figures I had heard last an year back. So the wife getting just 4 million and a duplex apartment is certainly a matter lost for her.

So Johnny now would be living all alone in his mansion at Bandra I think to myself.

I go to see him again at the same Shamiana resto and we sit, talk and eat like new lovers. Love is in the air again. I still don't ask him about his wife as I don't feel it is the right time yet and he too doesn't say anything about it. So I let it be that way considering that the information anyway is pretty confidential and me saying it to him would make him doubt the source of it, maybe that wouldn't be great for the friends of Mini who tipped the gossip to her. Though almost all of the showbiz industry likes to have tons of gossip for the breakfast everyday.

At the end after him paying the bill as usual to show who still the boss is, he out of the blue asks me to come to his mansion. It quickly shocks me, he actually caught me right of guard, doesn't even wait for my reply and pulls my hand with him in the backseat of his car saying

"Let your car be here, my driver will drop you right here whenever you leave"

I don't know why I don't even feel like rejecting his invitation and in fact a part of me just wants to do willingly what he tells me to, so with a smile I get in the car.

And we don't talk much during the drive as either

of us look out from the windows from our side. Seeing the beautiful Bombay from the windows is always soul pleasingly satisfying. The rush, the crowd, the traffic, the closeness of the congestion on the streets between the people and the cars, the hustle bustle filled with energy and life. Everybody seems restless as if nobody has got a fixed particular destination to reach ever. Until we reach near his mansion at the Bandstand Bandra and its all quite and almost empty with silence. Less people in extravagant places of the rich. Just a very few people standing far off to his mansion, they might be the fans. The crazy jobless ones. The windows of our car are totally black tinted from outside so that none can see who comes in there. But some of them are so hardcore of a fan that they would even recognize the vehicle of the star.

Once inside the cosiness of the house, he offers me a drink and then directly takes me upstairs, he doesn't talk even now as he pulls my hand into his lavish bedroom and then puts his palm right behind my lower back and quickly pulls me close to his body with my breast pressing hard on his strong chest. So close he is to me now that I can smell his too familiar breath. He then starts to greedily kiss me and before I can even resist him, he has his both hands firmly planted on my buttocks to pick me up in his strong arms as I make soft suppressed moans and then suddenly throws me hard on the large bed of his as I land on my back. That's when even he himself realizes how much I need and crave him.

He then gets over me while adjusting his hips by spreading my legs and starts to slowly thrust his pelvis between my thick soft thighs. Eventually he picks up a good speed and before I can push him away, he bends down to kiss my cheeks and thrusts himself harder inside me as all I can do now is to wrap my legs around his waist and my hands around his bare back moaning with holy pleasure.

He fucks me as much as he wants to and I can now feel all my anger, hatred and frustration towards him going far away with each tender passionate kiss of his on me. As I get an orgasm all the hatred that has been building up for months inside of me for him just disappears completely. I have surrendered myself to him, I am all of his to take. My Lucifer, My Lover. Fuck the world and it's things, he is my everything and the only thing I need.

CHARLES

L ying down through the cold night in my personal VIP torture prison cell with the thick metal chains through the wall still hanging loose wrapped around my ankles and wrists. I can now not even my feel any pain in my body since for every thing there is a limit. A certain limit to every fucking thing in the world. But these foolishly angry prison guards don't understand that, because they have beaten me so much more than my body can handle and now I can't even feel any pain nor can move a muscle without groans of agony and struggle. I am just numb and this paralytic feeling will continue till they again start bashing their instruments of violence on me.

But now I guess they actually are having a different limit set in their mind, that limit isn't about coping with how much my body can handle, but instead they maybe working in a limit till which they can beat and abuse without killing me for good. Honestly I would have died by now succumbing to my innumerable injuries and wounds, but it is the memory of Layla that keeps me going. I am all broken and fucked, but the thought of her is what fills me up with life again. The excessive soreness and ache doesn't even let me sleep much in the nights, so to ease my suffering I just relive in my mind the few yet priceless moments spent with her, the touch the feel, the body, the eyes. Every single thing I can remember about her in deepest depth.

So eventually it is the dusk and soon as the sharp sun rays from the top opening space fall on my face, I get up when I hear more footsteps approaching towards me, It feels odd. Since the footsteps towards my this isolated deserted torture cell are only heard late at night when they come to enjoy themselves by devastatingly trash me. But this early hour of the morning two guards get in and pull the chain on the wall to tighten it around my wrists, ankle and neck which forces me to stand upright on its support. I can look at the soaked blood of mine on the floor where I have been sleeping for these four nights since the prison fight.

So a prison head official who is a short but bulky man with an arrogant ugly face comes towards me in the cell and directly orders

"I need you to sign on a paper which would testify and act as a proof that that whore bitch actress was letting you fuck in this prison."

He waits for my reply and so does the other two guards standing at my either side, none say a word for a moment until I then give a slight smile as the prison official in front of me waits for my reply.

Then to his astonishment I break into a laughter at his foolishness. He feels offended for sure, but yet again tries to ask

"Or else you could say it verbally what we will beforehand have written for you and we will record your statement on a voice machine. That too would be an evidence enough for us and for your part, I can personally promise you, there will be no more gruesome torture on you and the rest of the years left in your prison time would be made smoother. What do you say?"

"No" I don't waste even a second to give my answer

"What did you say? I didn't hear" he asks again as if giving me another chance to correct my mistake

"I said fucking No" I reply energetically with all the little energy I have left in my bruised up body

"See, you will anyway have to testify against her, one way or the other, either you do it now peacefully cooperating with me as I say now and I will make sure everything will be better for you from now on" he says and pauses with a change in expression as now trying to conflict terror through it

"Or we would beat you until you do, we will force it out of you like we usually do with the others. The choice is yours. Take your time and think about it. I will ask you again at night." He turns and leaves through the opened metal gate of my cell as the guards then again loosen the chains as I fall hard on the cement bloody floor, they lock the metal gate of the cell and leave.

 I lay down fucked up on the crispy cement floor filled with the puddle of my dried maroon blood and then hours later a guard slides a thin steel plate towards me through the little space at the bottom of the cell door. I try and struggle to get my body anyhow to sit up to eat and I see just two hard pieces of bread which even though are the hardest ones I ever had, it doesn't even take me a minute to finish them. A hungry man would eat just anything to extinguish the evil fire of hunger in his stomach. Starvation is the worst kind of torture.

 Then I again lay down as sitting up for a long time with all the bruises and wounds on my body is not possible, also with the chains tied around my neck and limbs, it makes them tighter when I am doing anything rather than just lying flat on the ground like a dead man.

So as I lay down, until evening it is then that the realization dawns upon me when I do the assumption that the prison official was asking me for a written or a voice recorded audio of me personally in which I would testify mine and Layla's prison romance, so that these prison officials can use that to defame her and fuck her reputation in the eyes of the whole world by spreading these news, doing something so bad to her would be like kind of a revenge for these prison guards and officials against Layla for hurting their mean self esteem by not giving a fucking damn about them and just loving me with all her heart.

 I feel that until now maybe most probably they would have already tried to spread the news in the media about her affair with me, but then she obviously would have denied them all to be false allegations and rumours being casted upon her. By doing this all the bad news about her would have been considered baseless and since couldn't have affected her star image and reputation much. So this bastard cops are now trying to force me to give my statement as a confirmation of our affair, and then they would have substantial proof and more fuel in their news and allegations against her, thus they would be easily abled to fucking ruin her reputation and even the media outlets will again be able to run more juicy news about her, but that is only possible if I confess myself tonight.

 It's late at night and I am again almost asleep as the lack of strength in my body makes me dizzy as hell almost all the time now. The usual routine, the cell door is opened with the squeaking sound of the metal, I am straightened up by the tightening of the chains around me as the guards pull it by the wall and then the merciless torture. My deep long wounds and cuts after a night's torture usually swell and dry up a bit until the next day, when again I am beaten up on the same places as my wounds and cuts open up once again with wet fresh blood making it a feast for the mosquitoes and flies in here.

Everything is same as it has been for the last four days since I met Layla and the big fight in the prison broke out. Except there is one thing different this time as the prison guards around me are all ready to my bash me up as they stand with their whips and batons, but first the prison official who came to see me in the morning appears again now, asking me to testify against her and accept our prison love story. For a few good seconds, I just look at him and don't say a word, there is a complete nervous silence among all present in my cell now, and then I grin big with my bloody teeth looking in the waiting eyes of the prison official in front of me as I proudly with as much arrogance I can, say loudly

"Fuck Off! Suck my dick"

"Lawda Mera"

And I laugh, laugh like an evil, laugh like a free man, because after that I know that there is going to be a punishment for me like never before. They already were enough pissed and furious at me until now, but this arrogant behaviour of mine is like putting more fuel on the already burning hot flames of their hatred towards me. So after that senior prison official angrily and disappointingly leaves my cell, that is exactly what the three guards around me with their oiled whips and batons do to me. So intensely and gruesomely they hurt me this time, that soon I don't even realize when I fall unconscious due to the unbearable pain and the extreme weakness. They might just kill me, pretty soon. But I would love to die a death as painful as this with love for my lover in my loving heart as a testament to the the fact that even all the evil hate and force of the men of this world couldn't break me.

LAYLA

He then moves away from over me his sweaty naked body and then lights up a cigarette after we have made love twice till now today. He smoke a few puffs and then passes me his cigarette like the old times. This is the third time I have come to visit him at his Mansion in the last five days. Every time I have to park my car a little away from here and get into the mansion through the hideous small backside gate which is right in front of an almost empty and deserted type of lane since this particular lane is the road which is backside to even the surrounding smaller mansions near to Johnny's.

It is Johnny himself who requests me to park away and get in through the back door so that not a soul sees me getting in his house, the main enemies of ours would be the Paparazzi photo guys, those would make any uncomfortable picture viral and weave out a story from it for the audiences in whatever way they like. More than that it fucks with me that it is the audiences who are so naive to believe almost anything they are fed with no matter how nonsensical it might be.

Aah, who am I to judge, It is not even been a

month since Johnny's wife left him and here I am on his marital bed letting him fuck me even after all that he has made me go through.

 He is a Devil, the Devil, someone who would for sure end up in the worst of the Hell, but he is the Devil whom I have given my Heart and Soul to unfortunately. And he will definitely make sure to burn and melt them along with himself when the time comes.

 I even wear a big black scarf around my head and put on my usual big goggles, basically I try to cover myself as much as I can while entering his mansion so that even if someone sees me, I would be totally unrecognizable as the now infamous actress Layla Rathod and instead would look like just any random female or friend or maybe some Lawyer or Assistant of Johnny Singh entering his house.

 I pass the now more than half smoked cigarette to Johnny by my side as he keeps looking at the dark brown ceiling high above the bed, for a moment I too join him in looking above as we keep lying comfortably inside the thick white sheets naked. There is something going on in his mind for sure, that I can tell because obviously the ceiling is not that interesting to look at. The notoriety of my Lucifer? Then as he takes the last puff of the cigarette almost feeling a burn on his upper lip, he extinguishes it on the glass ashtray on the lamp table next to his side of the bed and speaks to me.

"There is a movie coming, Vikram Jha is directing it, it's like a big budget war romance film set in something 1600. I am the lead of course." he says while still with his gaze fixed on the ceiling as I look at him with adoration and then reply

"Wow, that's great. Really great. Vikram and You are always a perfect super hit combination The fans would go crazy." I say with a gentle smile and then he slowly turns his face to look into my eyes to say

"The heroine opposite me is a young new comer, she is the nephew of that old actor Sushant Gupta. But even though this girl looks gorgeous, I have met her a few times, things just don't feel as if they click between us. So if you want, only for you, I can do some arrangements and maybe get you the role. What say?" he says with an arrogant sparkle in his eyes which makes me feel as if he is trying to show me that I am nothing right now and that he is doing me a big favor like a Powerful Godfather by helping me out for this role. But I don't show any of my hard feelings and instead just smile at him and answer

"Sure, that would be so great Darling"

He smiles back at me and then again gets on top of me, wrapping his arm around my neck and kissing me all over again.

Johnny passionately and wildly touches every part of me, the worst and best part of it is that I never feel any love coming from him and in those touches of his, it just seems like he is an addict of my body savoring himself with every curve of it. Just an animal fulfilling his basic primal need of extreme lust. But I feel and enjoy the energy that gets into my skin upon his every touch as I close my eyes and give in myself to him fully always. That's when I remember Charles, my stranger prisoner. Even though I am and have always been in love madly with Johnny, I still cannot get Charles out of my messed up mind. I remember him often because there is no one who had ever looked at me the way he did, no one touched my body and soul together the way he did, no one ever made pure gentle love mixed with an extreme madness like him to me, there was something very different about him, and that something is what that would never let me forget him, My Guardian Angel, The Lover who would fight with the Worlds and the Hells Just for me.

For the first time ever, I am distractedly thinking about Charles while getting fucked by Johnny. The Heart is a Fool and the brain does not feel enough to be that clever. Alas none can help to make a sensible and logical decision.

CHARLES

In a dark room next to the courtyard, in a cardboard box, they give me back my civilian clothes. I put them on and realize that the clothes have been washed and ironed as there's not even a spot of blood of any guys I had killed in these clothes before coming in here. My wounds have dried up and healed pretty much, I was concerned initially about them getting infected bad, but a doctor took care of it well and good. As I walk though the courtyard, my heartbeat goes faster and soon as I reach the entrance gate of the prison, a guard opens it for me and before I can even realize and understand what's happening, I am already a free man standing on the concrete street outside the prison cell with a palm of mine covering my eyes since the sun today just feels too brighter and hotter than usual. I struggle to open my eyes fully with the mighty sun flaunting itself in front of me while hurting my soft eyesight with its sharp boiled rays, but then I see a person standing a little away in front of me on the other side of the street.

I try to focus and it seems like a woman, blooming around her an enchanting aura. More focus and it looks like a very pretty female, the best part is that she too is looking towards me and smiling. I start to take my steps towards her and eventually I spot her convertible roofless maroon muscle car next to her, I reach near the woman wearing a sleeveless bright red frock with small white circle spots on it and a big creme hat with a thin blue ribbon on it. I quickly recognize her as my love Layla Rathod, the most beautiful woman in the world. The Woman of my Dreams and the Woman of my Reality, the Keeper of my Heart and the Comfort of my Soul. She grins widely showing her shiny white teeth and I can't get my hands of her perfectly formed body as I hug her tight. The attractive sight of the glossy red lipstick on her fuller lips please me and I get stuck upon them for a moment as if they demand my whole attention. A heavenly feeling when she hugs me back tighter. We share a greedy kiss and a smile, then hop into her maroon muscle car as I wonder how is it even allowed to have such a perfect set of teeth.

 She takes me to her huge luxurious duplex apartment where we have just entered into it and she pulls me into her bedroom. We kiss with an intensity so great that we would soon chew the flesh of the other's tongue. I almost bite her lower lip and then we both can feel the celestial bittersweet taste of her hot blood in our mouths. That in fact makes us kiss and get into each other's mouths more ferociously.

 The immense heat of love from our bodies makes us sweat with passion of such kind as if we would be stuck and glued onto each other forever after this ethereal moment.

 As we reach near the bed, I quickly turn her around with her curvy back now facing me and I as usual start to softly kiss my lips on the side of her thin fragile smooth neck. Slowly my kisses descend till her deep collarbone and then I unzip the red frock of hers and throw it away as I keep caressing and touching her, playfully exploring her body, softly and subtly feeling her sensitive breasts as she turns putty in my hands. Sooner she is bent on the bed on her knees and I stand behind on my feet and then. We Fuck with Love. We Fuck for Love. Making Love was a thing of the past for us, a thing we did in the confined walls of the prison. But today we weren't making love, today we are just unleashing our wild passions for each other, after all today we were as free as the animals of any jungle and even fucking with the heat and fire like theirs. Mixed and Merged like two totally different shades of paint color on a Canvas.

 Wonderful days of life like these kind went on and on after that, we would often fuck nice until there would be not even a hint of energy left in our youthful bodies, then she would lit up a cigarette and we would smoke that together before she would go to sleep with her beautiful head on my chest and I would just stay awake watching the innocent angelic face of hers, my Layla looking so Perfect that always it would make me wonder if I even deserve her?

 That's the thing about life, it's always all about Abundance, when you got pain and suffering in your time, it is in abundance, when you got fail-ures, endless struggles and heartbreaks, it is in abundance too, It is rule of the Nature to bestow upon man whatever it wants to but only in Abun-dance. But also it is an another rule of nature to Change no matter what, so the time passes no matter what, the good becomes bad and the bad becomes good no matter what, Time passes and everything changes, the one at the cruel bottom of the wheel doesn't even realize how and when suddenly he gets to the highest top of the wheel and vice versa, the sufferings and struggles turn in to love and immeasurable success. Then that too is in fucking Abundance.

 The hand which would turn to Stone whatever it touched, now suddenly becomes a hand that could make anything it touches Gold.

 Some days she would even make food for us, nor-mally it would be the maids in her home that would cook, but some days in a romantic mood, My Layla would cook something delicious for me to show her love even though she is good at and well versed at the recipe of only a couple of dishes, still with her pretty limited cooking abilities as she would stand at the kitchen counter wearing shorts and extra large comfy t-shirts of mine with her brunette hair tied back loosely in a bun, I would often go behind her and hug her by wrapping my strong arms around her fragile body while kissing her soft cheeks with my naughty hands running over pressing her perfectly formed round breasts. Then as my hands would then slid down to caress her curvy buttocks, she would then move away the dishes and the ingredients from the kitchen table to the side and then turn herself around to eat my face with a smile. I would lift her and put her on the kitchen table and as always we would fuck passionately until we would be tired enough to fall down on the floor with no ounce of energy left in our tired sweaty bodies. Fuck till Failure, that was our oath. Then she would normally continue cooking the favorite dishes if she still got the mood and vibe, or else we would just order something from outside, either of which we would relish together with cups of red wine and wonderful soothing music playing on an antique vinyl record player. We would Laugh and Love. Time goes fast, but it has no power over Love. Love can be Endless and Infinite.

My Ex Boss Karim Lala calls me one particular day, summons me to his place and after our formal show of affection with hugs, handshakes, cuisines and drinks to celebrate our reunion and meeting after so long, asks me about when will I be coming back to work, to which I instantly refuse in the most polite way possible. To my surprise he takes my response good and respectfully accepts my decision of not coming again to kill people for him in an understanding way. Immediately accepts the answer and doesn't even try pushing me. Even though in the most polite and the softest way, still the straightforward refusal of mine to work for him even quite surprises me as he Karim Lala has been more than a Father to me, A true Godfather, he brought me up all the way from rags and even if I think that I have evened out and settled the score by killing all those men all those years in his service, I would still be indebted to him endlessly forever as he is the sole reason for me making it well and alive all the years of growing up, I survived just because of his protective palm on my head. Without his support I would have been nothing. So he is the one person to whom I thought and never would have wanted to refuse and say a no to, but Until Today. I am a Changed Man. Love Changes Everything and Everone. No wonder it is the most Powerful Force and Feeling in the Whole of the Universe. After that day, my great Saint didn't even bother me, he was wise and sweet enough to just keep in touch by sometimes sending us expensive presents only on Eid and other selective festivals. That maybe was a way of his to show that a part of him was somewhat guilty that he couldn't help me out in my time at the prison.

Some days Layla would take me to her Large

Extravagant movie sets as a spectator where she would introduce me to everyone as her Boyfriend, her new found true love, and the majority of them, if not all, would just look at me confused thinking how in the world possibly could a nobody guy with average looks like mine had managed to get such a gorgeous diva to fall in love with him. So judgemental they would be, but fuck it, I shouldn't and wouldn't care, for the ones who are going to judge you are always going to judge you anyways.

 Then for the long taxing hours of the shooting I would sit on my chair and watch her working, I would often see the lead actors opposite her getting too close, touchy or intimate with her during the scenes and I would feel jealous. But never would I show it on my face or in any expressive way. I am Possessive. Too much Possessive about her Maybe. But I know that this is her work and all that romantic heart touching stuff she says to those other actors in those movies with tears in her eyes is all fake bullshit and just acting. What startles and amazes me is that she is one of those greater actors who won't even need glycerin to get that burning sensation in the eyes which would then produce the fake tears, here she actually in the deepest way feels the pain of the character she is playing and then starts to sob. The Art of Acting, when perfected can make anyone seem as if it is the reality of that person being portrayed. But it is the "Cut" sound of the director which acts as my saviour as that's when she and the actors instantly come out of their extraordinarily believable acts and would just light up a cigarette and chat like just any normal co-workers with the makeup artists doing more touch ups on their already touched upon many time faces. The way these actors transition in and out of their roles smoothly like the switch of a button with such ease, scares me quite a bit.

One day she introduces me to one of her directors of a movie and before I know, I am an Action Choreographer and a Stunt Man in the movie business.

The job actually is a pretty soothing enjoyable walk in the softest garden, as the movie business and all its violence and gore is fake as fuck. Here I have by now been through, seen, and made so many others feel real "brick shitting" pain in their lives. The fights which I choreograph here and be a part of when necessary are just too flashy and way exaggerated kind of stuff which would be more than just impractical in real life situations. But in front of the camera after all we are just performing a performance, so practicality and common sense just leaves the place right away once the director says "Action" and the big camera starts rolling. Here with time I learned it the hard way that only what looks Good is what Sells Good. Even the stunts which seem like a total daredevilry which

I do as a stunt double for the pussy hero of the movie is just a glimpse of what I had and used to do in my career as a legit Serial Killer. Nobody appreciates me after the extraordinary work and skills I showcase because it is for the hero guy who has no courage and balls to do his own stunts , the one getting away with all the credit, applause, hoots, whistles, good pieces of ass and what not. Such Foolish audiences. But fuck it, I don't care and I shouldn't, the Money is Good. Fat as fuck.

 A year in love with her and she gets blessed with a child in her womb. Even though I personally don't want her to, I still think that she would maybe just abort or drop the child. Being at the peak of your career in the movie business and having a baby in your tummy doesn't fit well maybe I thought, but to my surprise she makes the decision that we would have the baby no matter what and should moreover soon get married.

 The perfect time to tie the knot, just a few of her very close friends which are mostly the coworkers of the movie fraternity and even fewer than that some relatives of hers. None from my side, Kareem Lala is and has always been like a father to me, but now I wish to just be as far away as possible from that ugly contract killing business of his, so I guess not keeping much contact from my side with him is the only way to keep him at bay and not give him any ideas or hopes of me coming back, after all I was his number one guy. Anyway I just wouldn't want to call someone as dreaded as a Gangster like him to my private small wedding. That would make it too controversial. His presence in the wedding would attract unnecessary eyeballs and definitely would be a head turner.

I wear a full white tuxedo and she fills herself in the most gorgeous black silk gown which shined brighter than any diamond. As I stand at the stage seeing her arrive with her maids of honor, I like many times before, fell in love with her all over again. The Bollywood stars perform in our wedding and even at the next ceremony the day after this.

Life is all good, A baby girl it is, The most beautiful little thing in the world it is. Maria is what we have named her. Soft, Chubby she is and dark almond eyes she got. Nose like Layla and just a hint of me on that face. She only looks like me when she is crying, or else whole of the time and all her features are an exact replica of Layla, no wonder she is the most beautiful baby in the world, after all she looks like her mother who is a very celebrated movie actress and a part time Fairy in the Heavens. I am in fact happy she only looks a tiny bit like me.

Maria is great, the best thing ever happened to me after Layla, except she just doesn't let us ever sleep. Making love has just been a thing of the past for us since an year now. This time I actually mean it, as even passionate fucking of ours has stopped. Now Maria baby would like a demanding boss get up at any hour of the night and cry until any of us would take her in the arms and walk in the home. The girl just wouldn't stop crying in the hands of the maids. How in the world possibly can a infant so small realize and recognize which of the people and blood is of her own? Quite astonishes me and things like is what makes me consider Believing in God. So it is mostly me who then comes to take her in my arms from the maid since Layla anyway gets too tired by taking care of her the whole day. The baby just sleeps a very few hours, like tiny power naps to recharge itself to wake up and cry loudly at the top of its lungs to make us take her up in the arms and walk. Just a few more months and Layla would start to go out to continue work and her previous movie commitments. I too have some commitments to complete on other movie projects. Until now we are both on vacation and have taken a long holiday for our sweet darling Baby Maria.

 Layla is sleeping in the bedroom peacefully like some Snowwhite and I am walking in the living room with lovely Maria in my arms, her tiny round head supported on my shoulder while taking utmost care of her soft fragile neck by keeping my hand behind her head, I think that obviously pretty soon we will have to hire even a Nanny for her. That nanny lady would be way more experienced and better in handling infant children than these maids of the house ever would, because that is what she does for a living, her profession. So I guess even the baby would be more easy and comfortable with her. Only then we will be able to go out to work if we have some one professional like that to look after our little sweetheart Baby girl. Or maybe it is at least going to be an another six months until Layla would consider going out since she has to breastfeed the baby. I don't know, let's see how things unveil with time, but I am sure excited and overwhelmed by all this. Slowly I am realizing that it is infact the one and only point of life, to be Happy. And for the first time in my long life, I can say with total confidence and without the slightest fear of things going haywire, that I actually am Happy.

As I am busy in my thoughts I realize that by now Maria is asleep. I slowly walk towards the bedroom and with extreme tenderness I descend to keep the baby next to her sleeping mother. I do this act of descending and keeping her back on the bed with the slowest of the movements because if the baby realizes even a hint that she is being kept back down from the arms, she would again get awake and cry causing havoc until her mother would then maybe feed her.

I do succeed in keeping her below on the bed without waking her up, but it disturbs the sleep of Layla a bit. I too then lie on my side of the bed. A perfect moment it is for me, the wonderful cutest baby of ours just right in the centre of the bed between us and my hand caressing softly the cheeks of Layla to make her fall asleep too, while I just place my long index finger at the centre of the little open palm of my asleep baby which she soon wraps her softest tiny fingers around it. Damn, I love my family so much, what not in the world would I do for them?

Feeling the luckiest and the most cherished man in the world, I smile like a fool knowing very well that this is the happiest I have ever been in my whole life and with that gratitude, love and smile on my face, I too close my eyes and soon fall asleep with my family. Aah, yes, My Family.

An annoying striking sound of a metal, high enough to destroy my sleep and I open my eyes to my reality. I am still laying down in the dried up pool of my own wasted blood in the torture jail cell of mine I soon realise with the tears in my eyes and black blood in my veins that it was all just an impossible dream. A too beautiful perfect dream, perfect enough to be just a dream.

That is the thing about dreams, while dreaming you do not realize that you are fucking dreaming and that everything around you actually is just an illusion. It only dawns upon you it was a dream when you wake up to the harsher reality.

Two guards are unlocking and opening the metal

gate of my prison cell, the noise of them clank-ing their steel baton on the metal rod of my cell door would have most probably been the sound that woke me up in this hell of a reality so rudely transitioning me from the loveliest paradise of a dream. Gosh! what not what I do for that sweetest dream to come true. Even if it would mean the im-possible task to Kill all the Professional Hitmen and the Top Assasins of the world, I would still give it a shot, because even the thought of it hav-ing just the tiniest chance of success to live that dream life would be enough to make it all worth the try. But Alas! Nothing like that is going to happen and there is nothing I can and should do to achieve that Dreamy Heavenly Life. I should in fact stop thinking about her and keeping even the slightest of the expectations. Expectations are such a bitch, they always hurt way more brutally than a sharp knife stabbed inside your flesh ever would.

 Coming to an agreement with my Reality, I start sobbing and breaking like a little boy, with mucus coming out of my nose and fresh tears running over my cheeks, I cry with a terrible pain in my voice as they tighten the chains on the walls to pull my body up. They seem a bit frightened and puzzled at first but then smile at each other assuming that the pain in my cry would be be-cause of the suffering, wounds and the tortures of the prison which they and other officers have bestowed upon me. But the actual reason for my psychotic crying like a "devil losing a son" is because of the deeper understanding of the fact that all I had just dreamed was not only a dream, but it is a dream which would never actually be a Reality. Never. Even if I would move the mountains and tear the sky, this dream of being and living a life of love with Layla will Never be a Reality. It will always just be an incomplete dream which I will always cherish as a memory. A treasure of a memory. A memory that would even hurt like a heated sword if cherished for too long.

They once again start to force me with all their power to give my statement and sign against Layla, which of course I don't They keep hitting me with their sticks, asking me repeatedly to do the deed and I keep refusing.

"Just sign on that paper Goddamit !" shouts one of them getting restlessly annoyed while hitting me on my bruised back

"Why don't you just follow our orders and do what we tell you to?" said another while losing his thin patience and giving me another hard hit.

I just flinch hard with the pain and then move my head sideways to disagree with them.

"Why don't you accept the real fact in front of the world that Layla Rathod was letting you fuck her in this prison? Why is it so difficult for you to do it you bastard? She is a whore and do you like getting bashed in here for a whore? Or even then are you putting yourself foolishly through all this pain just in the name of Love? Are you crazy enough to think she would be in love with you? You piece of shit, she is such a big Superstar, she would not even be giving a damn about you now, she can have a hundred more men like you with all that money and fame of hers. In fact even right now as you are getting tortured like a dog in this cell in her love, she right now might be on somebody else's bed." says the guard almost trying to befriend me with his subtler tone and then he comes close to my bloody face and looks into my red bloodshot eyes saying in a calm sympathetic voice

"You will sign the papers would you? You aren't that crazy to die for a whore right?"

I glance at my unrecognizable and almost dead beaten up reflection of mine in his dark wide opened eyes and then I burst into a big laugh. A laugh big enough with a tone to offend the fuck out of him. Just for this moment I once again feel like a free man as I cunningly laugh to my heart's fill while looking at the ceiling of my cell as the sudden burst of laughter makes the blood collected in my mouth unintentionally spit on his face, but I would not care less and I continue to enjoy the spirit of my laughter. So then the face of that guard starts to boil red furiously and with humiliation, he lifts his baton and as if the devil himself has taken control over him, he lands a pretty hard blow right on the top of my forehead almost cracking my skull.

I do not know if he has cracked open a vein or pierced through my skin or fractured the bone of skull because honestly I did not feel a thing from the quick unexpected blow from the swing of his baton stick. But then instantly after the monstrous hit as he keeps talking or maybe shouting at me, I soon feel the sound of reality and existence being pulled away from my ear drums with a burning sensation in them, its all gradually going mute. Now not only can I not hear but even my vision starts to get blurry with each silent blink of my eyes, everything has slowed down, even the movements and the gestures of the furious officer. Pretty soon the noiseless ghost and blurry oil painting like outline figure of the police officer in front of me eventually disappears, all I have got then in front of me is blackest darkness. The beautiful ethereal darkness which pulls me into itself and all my pain and sorrows go numb. I free fall but quite slowly and delicately as this eternal world of darkness seems like an infinitely large vacuum into which I am endlessly falling and falling. My body dives deep into the depths of this world of vacuum and as the darkness around me begins to fill itself in my aching body, all my cuts, my lost blood, my wounds, my broken heart gets replaced with the grand darkness of this surreal blackest world.

 Am I dead yet? Maybe, maybe not. But I can feel my soul already starting to numbly leave from my feet up to my torso, my hands and eventually leading up to my head. The immense weight of the soul feeling in my head as if it just wants to get out bursting through the top of my skull smashing through my brain into pieces. Or maybe I am not dying, I am just unconscious and my whole body numb as fuck for now except for my head, as the excruciating pain in my skull would be the latest wound from the hit of the baton which the fellow officer had given me a moments ago.

 I am all unconscious but can now feel everything. I am the most Dead and Awake at the same time.

 Then I hear someone appearing at my cell gate whispering something, making weird noises from his mouth as if calling me, there is a kind of an urgency and fear in his voice which I can easily sense that makes me open my eyes wide while lying like a dead man in blood on the prison floor and I look up at him. It is a short heighted prisoner who is thin in frame and bald at the centre of the head, looking here and there nervously to check at the guards around and still making suppressed noises and whistles from his mouth to wake me up. Have I seen this guy before? maybe I have. Or maybe not, I can not recognize him much. As soon as he sees me trying to get up, while standing outside he puts one hand of his into my cell through the gap between the metal rods and in his hand out of no where appears a white envelope which he then throws it instantly towards me. Before I can even pickup the envelope and ask that prisoner any-thing, he is long gone. Just vanished into thin air like the Dark Knight.

I pick up the envelope abruptly not giving it the chance to get all messed up wet and soaked in the blood on the floor. I nervously tear it to open and take out the piece of paper in it, a letter it is of course. But who in the world would write me a letter now? Would it be my Boss and Godfather Karim Lala? Obviously he can not come to prison to see me, but still he does not strike me as a per-son who would write a letter to me if he needed to pass on a thought or a message of his to me. He might have send a man of his to talk to me during the relatives visiting hours of the jail or some hired lawyer. So with all the uneasy curios-ity building up inside of me, I open up the thick slick white paper of smooth high quality and start to read the letter under the strong rays of the sun coming in from the above window-like space of my cell.

Dear Charles

Deep in my heart I know that I can hope, just hope

and only helplessly hope that this letter finds you in good health and condition, or after what I had seen last, expecting the letter to even just find you would be quite demanding and maybe too much to ask for.

But even if by the slightest chance of God's grace it does, then all I can say is "Take care and may that Sweetest God Bless You".

You know who I am and I just wanted you to know that whatever you think we had was all just a thing of the moment or moments you could say. And to be honest, they were good moments. A treasure. They were very much like the fairy tale moments I act in the scenes of the movies. Knowing fully that once the scene is called to be Cut by the director, there is no more life and realism left in those moments no matter how hard I tried to believe in them truthfully during the act. Alas the insides of that treaure box are just fakes coated with cheap shiny metals.

The reason for this letter is to make you understand the truth, the reality, that there wasn't ever anything between us. All it was or we thought it would be, was all a big mistake and just too good to be true type of fantasy.

I have found someone now and I intend to spend the rest of my life with him, though I don't even need to tell you anything more, I just am saying this so that it becomes clear in your head and heart that nothing like Love and foolish stuff of that kind was or will ever be between you and I. It was all a terrible mistake. A crime for which we both have and are being punished in our own ways.

They say that when a Man and a Woman are alone in a room, the Devil too is present in the same room who makes them do the deeds of passion which they would later regret.

If anyone asks anything, just say you never talked to me. Other than that everything else will be taken care of.

I would never ever see you again and I hope you do good in life once you get out of the prison which again I hope you soon will.

LAYLA

It is a sunny morning and I am standing in my balcony having a smoke, front of me a spectacular view of the artistic beautiful clouds in the sky. Just a few white clouds in the large endless light blue of the sky. The monsoon is over and the water on the streets have by now all dried up, road side shops of all kinds will now be lively open more than ever.

Just a month more and winter will be there, but just a slight cold winter. The good better part of winter will be three months later from now during the Christmas and New Year's eve. But as compared to all the other places, it is never ever too cold here in Bombay. A person could get through his whole life without wearing a jacket or a sweater in the Bombay climate.

I am almost at the bottom of my cigarette and next thing I would be doing would be to take a quick shower and visit Ramnath Studios in Andheri since I have got preparations, contracts, meetings and scripts to do for my role in the movie Johnny just got me into. Four days later from today we would start shooting the movie, principal photography.

Meanwhile I take a last puff of my cigarette and once again feel the quick intense burn of the cigarette butt in the flesh of my upper lip. It often happens that when I get so much involved and pre-occupied in my thoughts, deep inside the world of my mind, I often over smoke the cigarette more than it is meant to be which is reaching till the butt where as mostly normally when I am consciously aware, I would smoke just two-third of the cigarette and just stub it off, not good for the lips to smoke it till the very bottom end they say. The tiny yet soul shaking burn on the lip makes me agree with that fact so much more.

Is it guilt? Maybe just a way to punish myself to listen to my heart then or to not to listen to my heart now?

The reason for these tiny burns are always me getting utterly lost deep in the maze of my thoughts and right now I was thinking about him. The Stranger Prisoner who fell in love with me, and maybe even I did, Charles was his name as far as I remember. Nothing more than that to the name he said and because I guess I did not even ask, so he did not bother to. I still don't know for what crime is he serving time in the prison, but I honestly feel deep inside my heart that he certainly would have not done anything that bad to innocent people. He of course seems like a deadly killer, the way he killed some and fought those other stupid prisoners in the jail and that big guy trying to get his hands on me. So he knows how to kill and in a very professional way, it is his profession it seems. But I can bet for sure that he would kill and attack only the bad guys and never ever lay his murderous hands on an innocent soul. But God knows, I may even be wrong, it just might be the movie world of mine that is making me think like that about him and justify his unforgivable crime of murder. I don't fucking know anything about him honestly, it is just the love for him in my heart that might be making me soft for him, for he maybe the worst killer of all. He might just be any Serial Killer who would kill anyone for the right amount of cash. Maybe even me someday, if the amount is good enough.

But I am clever, I know I have always been. So I wrote that letter to him. I don't know if he is actually a good or a bad person and I should not even care, because the wise thing obviously would be to end it with him whatever it was. So even though is a substantial risk of my letter getting caught by the cops inside and then they will easily use it against me and all the rumours and news about my affair would splash ugly on my face, though Mini made the best use of her contacts and influence to get the job done. At first mini totally refused and hesitated to do it, in fact she was not even going to let me do it, so when I out of anger assured her that no matter what, I would write that damn letter and make sure it reaches him even if I personally would have to go to give to him in prison, she then said she would take care of it. A shady friend of hers in construction business had some contact with the boy whose small tea shop is next to the prison site, this tea seller boy would often be called at least thrice a day into the prison for the cups of tea for the officers and hawaldaars, so there he passed on the letter to one of his recently befriended new prisoner who then in turn might have until now passed the letter to Charles. I do not know if he had received it yet or not, as there is no way of confirming it and can only hope that it does. Mini was clever enough to make the suggestion to not use my name or give out my identity directly in any way in the letter so that even if the letter gets caught in the hands of the police staff, I would then deny the letter being from me and have the lawyers use the legal loopholes and sue them police for falsely defaming me. There would not be any way of tracing it back to me, but still any person in that prison after what has happened will clearly and easily understand that it is me who has written the letter, but even then if caught, I can use the excuse that someone else might have written the letter just to get my name into trouble. A conspiracy to defame an actress.

I hope and just hope with all my heart that that letter reaches into the hands of Charles because it is the necessary closure for us, I do not want him to be thinking or have any hopes about us, it hurts to have them hopes. Hurts more when you later see those hopes shattering and not every one can handle that pain, so it is better to shatter the hopes sooner. Because any wiser person would know that there is no way that our love can ever be complete. It is just one of the many true yet incomplete love stories. Better to seal off and close the chapter until it ends in an irreversible tragedy.

 I then get off from the balcony and go back into the house, take a warm shower and a quick light breakfast before dressing up and leaving for my meeting at Ramnath Studios. Just below the building in the parking lot, next to my car, there is my lovely Mini already present waiting for me with a cups of Starbucks Coffee in her each hand, one for her and another for me, such an angel she is, even though I just had my two morning cups of black coffee, I still feel overwhelmed seeing the coffee in her hand, extra caffiene never hurt anyone. As I walk towards her, she is smiling with her white teeth, in her well fitted white blazer and pants over a thin light pink shirt, standing tall in her black heels next to my white BMW, she then gives me a hug. Her hugs always make me feel comfortable and calm. She is family after all. We get in the car and leave. The security guard of our Society as always does not forget to salute me even though I have obviously never asked him to as I drive off through the gate of our society hoping to go on to the smoother roads of the city and life.

CHARLES

T iny blood drops from my head start to fall on the white paper in my hand. The red fresh blood of mine pouring out through the thin crack or maybe a busted vein raining directly onto this letter which just broke me more badly than I could have ever imagined. But these blood drops are not the only thing that are dropping and getting soaked quickly into this letter of heartbreak, even my tears of immeasurable sadness are falling onto it. My hands are shaking more than they ever had, even more than when I had killed a person for the first time in my life. As far as I remember even they were not trembling as such, my Godfather Lala was quite impressed with the stiffness and coldness to my approach towards my victim. I was a Born Killer they said, but now not only my hands, but I feel that my whole soul is shaking like a tornado. My heart now feels like million shattered pieces of glasses, sharp glasses with the pointest edges which now are hurting and cutting up all the insides of me that comes into its contact. Is that what the doctor calls Internal Bleeding?

The blood drops falling on the crispy white paper look good bright red while hiding the blue ink text of the paper until my agony heavy tear drops too get mixed with it and now it is a faded pink coloured paper in my hands and soon the blue ink spreads and disappears into just a color mixed with the red. The excessive moist absorption soon makes the paper soft, fragile and weaker like my present state. A little movement and I am sure it will tear up. But I am not sure what will tear up first, My fragile heart, my shaken soul, my tested patience or this soft piece of wet paper.

Who would believe the power and the effect this wet piece of paper just had on one of the World's Deadliest Killer? I guess it is right when they say that the Pen is more powerful than the Sword.

As I move and tilt my body a little to the right, the sharp spear like long sunrays coming in my cell through the large space opening at the top of the wall of this prison, fall on my fragile wet letter and all of a sudden the blue pink color on white seems to shine bright like a thing of an another world. It looks magnificent and heavenly, so indescribably marvelous that with all the light shining around it makes it almost hurtful to a mortal's eye as if this was particularly written for me by an Angel above the Clouds. I just tear the letter instantly and furiously. No piece of paper should have that much power. Tear it up hurriedly into as many pieces as possible and shout with such intensity that the veins on the side of my neck would explode or even the ones going to my brain. It does make more blood pop out of my forehead cut though. I shout and shout until I am exhausted and put my head down on the floor. My body is exhausted but not my frustration. The lava boiling in me is fresh as fuck. To my surprise not a single police guard comes to quieten me. Or maybe it was not that surprising a thing after all, they do not actually give a damn about my state here anyway. The whole day bastards keep me lying like a dead mice rotting in the cell here and then at night is when they pull my chains up to torture my weakened body and toughened soul.

I sit calmly now looking at the small scattered pieces of paper of the letter which I just angrily tore. I pick up a piece to wipe up the blood coming out from the little wound or opening cut on the top of my forehead. Keep up a little pressure on it for a while assuming that it might stop. Majority of the wounds on my body anyway have now dried up, in a bad way, but still have dried up though I fear some of them might even be or get infected soon. But I know I am not going to die here, I had forgotten my goal for a while but now "She My Angel" has through this letter reminded me again. I had and have to escape this shithole prison and I definitely will.

What a fool I was to think that she could be mine, that such a big top superstar actress would be in love with me. Of course she was just having fun with me, letting me go mad over her, but it is hard to believe that she was playing along only for the sake of pleasure and thrill because I had seen it in her eyes. In her eyes the true love for me, the way she made love to me, it was not the kind which felt being just done for pleasure, it was as if recreating a new kind of unseen love in this planet, the love she had made to me felt like the declaration of the greatest type of love in the universe, or maybe it was all just fake. She is an actress after all and that too a good one, portraying fake emotions which look more than real is what she does for a living, acting is her profession, all she did might have been fake, her eyes lied to me to believe that she loved me like no one else on this earth have or would ever love someone. The same way she fools the audiences to believe in and sympathize with her characters in her movies.

 But she did a good thing, really smart and a clever thing to send this "directly from Hell" letter for me. Though it tore me and tortured my soul in unimaginable ways, it was a good thing for both of us. She made everything crystal clear. She is not an angel of the clouds but the witch of the dark underworlds. The witch really in fact did me a favour because now she had pulled me out of my dreamy fairy tale like love story and have put me cold heartedly right into the harsh reality of life. Faded away the illusion she had casted, what hurt the most was the suddenness and brutality of pulling away the blanket of fairytale illusion she had warmly covered me in. Made me open my eyes and just throw away the rose colored tinted glasses of love. Of course my eyes were meant to hurt experiencing so much darkness all at once of her Real world, the underworld. The witch I loved, the witch that made love to me as if I was the Lucifer.

Even if the letter has broken my heart, that does not mean that I would snitch on her now. I have and will always admire her. In fact I am glad that she found someone else, I am happy for her because when looked upon honestly and practically, there is no way she and me could anyway get together in life.

She now made me remember who I am, I am a killer, I love killing people, that is what I do. That is my fate and destiny - The two things which cannot be altered. I have always been a killer and will always be one. There no such thing as feelings and love for people like me in our lives. These kind of things only make us weak. Emotions are poisonous. I will get all this bullshit toxic stuff out of my head to just focus on the reality and the important stuff which is how to get out of here now. I will start observing again and figuring out another way even though I had failed miserably in my last escape attempt.

I will escape this shithole prison, I have to escape and for now I do not know how, but I definitely will. I have to escape. Sentence for life is a joke.

Fuck that Bitch. She played me.

But a part of me knows, The Love in her eyes for me was as Real as the God and the Universe.

If you Loved this book, then you will definitely love these other books from the Author

- **<u>The Interview With The Don</u>**
- **<u>The Thieves With Big Balls</u>**

ABOUT THE AUTHOR

Junaid Asif is a twenty one year old independent filmmaker who writes, directs, choreographs, edits and acts in his short films and music videos to post on YouTube. He even makes Vlogs and comedy skits. The reason behind writing this book is to sell this piece of fiction to raise money to make this into a full feature Action Romance movie.

The Author believes that Life is Suffering, but in that Suffering even if for a Moment He can Entertain and Distract people in the Best way possible from their stressful lives through his work, then the purpose of his existence will be fulfilled and the Goal of his life achieved.

So if you have read the book till here, then the author thanks you from the bottom of his heart and requests you to please either comment your feedback whatever good or bad it is on Amazon page comments or Dm me on my Insta please?

YouTube Channel – Junaid Asif Tube

Instagram – junaidasiftube

BOOKS BY THIS AUTHOR

The Interview With The Don

6 Brutal Years of Horrifying Crime the Bombay Mafia doesn't want you to know.

Thieves With Big Balls

Robbing someone as dreaded as the Don of Bombay Mafia is no joke